FONDLY

"Winnette's novellas are two separate exercises in absurdism… *Gainesville* moves like a serial killer in a getaway car, like life and death on fast-forward … in contrast to *In One Story, the Two Sisters* … where the situations are an endless, whimsical adventure to read."

—Christopher Allen, *Metazen*

"*Fondly* has a refreshingly distinct vision and voice that, at times, left me breathless. Winnette doesn't take any shortcuts. He pulls the reader into each character's life without preamble. On a sentence level he's playing with sharp hooks that embed the skin."

—Ben Spivey, *Heavy Feather Review*

"Colin Winnette was born in 1984, but he writes like he's either lived from birth to death once before, or else is only an unaffected observer, born immutable to time."

—Michael Davidson, author of *Austin Nights*

"Winnette communicates something that's true … facets of our existence that have become as basic as sun up and sun down."

—Kevin Morris, DBC|Reads

"What I love most … is Winnette's poetic glimpse of our own oblivion, and how he arrives there variously with post-postmodern sensibility."

—Joni Wallace, author of *Blinking Ephemeral Valentine*

REVELATION

"In *Revelation,* Colin Winnette sets fire to the world, and in the aftermath, characters wander through smoke, struck dumb by devastation. A forceful book—stripped down, cool and painful—about the absolute peril of desire." —Ben Marcus, author of *The Flame Alphabet* and *Notable American Women*

"Alternating the apocalyptic with the laconic, the end-of-times with the poignantly down-to-earth, *Revelation* is full of fine surprises. Colin Winnette has a sharp eye, a good ear, an ironic spirit and, like a smaller scale Terrence Malick, he's made a provocative work by framing the ordinary in the unfathomable." —Rosellen Brown, author of *Before and After* and *Civil Wars*

"Keep your eye on this Colin Winnette. He's a gifted stylist, and quite often a funny one." —Adam Levin, author of *Hot Pink* and *The Instructions*

"*Revelation* is a tremendous book worthy of every bit of acclaim it has already received and definitely a novel that should further help solidify Mutable Sound as an indie house to look out for." —J.A. Tyler, author of *No One Told Me I Was Going to Disappear* and *Variations of a Brother War*

ANIMAL COLLECTION

"What I loved about this story was its swift blunt movement—how one paragraph would move to the next without much transition and great bits of info would get revealed along the way. The quickness allowed for an emotional punch that I found very effective and powerful."

—Aimee Bender, author of *The Particular Sadness of Lemon Cake* and *The Girl in the Flammable Skirt*

"Amid psychological unease and disorienting sexual encounters, Winnette's characters throw garbage in rivers, contemplate divorce, circle aquariums, perform vivisection, battle and become vermin. Part Wes-Anderson-on-Beckett dioramas, part echo-boomer on Kafka dramaturgy, each piece works to shatter ontological constructs of what is human and what is animal. The tiny sparks that fly off each, strangers and charms, make up Winnette's trouble-wall called the human condition."

—Joni Wallace, author of *Blinking Ephemeral Valentine*

FONDLY

FONDLY

COLIN WINNETTE

An Atticus Trade Paperback Original

ATTICUS BOOKS

atticusbooks.net

Excerpts from *In One Story, the Two Sisters* appeared in *PANK* and *Word Riot,* and excerpts from *Gainesville* appeared in *Housefire.*

ISBN-13: 978-0-9840405-8-2
ISBN-10: 0-9840405-87

Page composition by David McNamara
Cover design by Walter Green
Drawings by Scott Teplin
Typeset in Bembo

IN ONE STORY, THE TWO SISTERS

In one story, the two sisters lived in the country and were in love with the same old man.

One sister was blind, the other couldn't walk, and the old man sometimes brought them milk and eggs and fish from town. They stopped him one day—he was delivering a two-day-old salted cod and a dozen eggs—and they asked for penicillin, a syringe, a box of bandages, some gauze, a calendar, and a handful of candies. The sister in the wheelchair lifted the hem of her younger sister's dress to expose a wound the size of a silver dollar just above her ankle. It was bleeding, and obviously infected.

I fell, said the blind sister.

The wheelchair-bound sister explained they didn't have any money for the cod or the eggs, but she swore they'd have something for him when he came back with the other supplies. The old man said he was glad to help, though he was suspicious of their promise to pay. It was a lot to ask, a lot of money for those supplies, which made it very different from occasionally stopping by with old fish.

He showed up the next day with the supplies and they took him out back, the wheelchair-bound sister leading the blind sister leading the old man, and they showed him an old oak tree all rotted out and big enough to fit a man or, as they had it, a whole stack of money left to them by their great-great-grandfather. They couldn't keep the money in the house, they said, because what if someone robbed them and raped them, then it would be as if they were paying the creature to do so. The old man listened to their explanation, and then they asked him to climb in and get the money.

We would do it, said the wheelchair-bound sister, *but she would have trouble feeling her way around in there, finding the stack, counting the money, and I haven't got the length of arm to reach inside and grab your payment.*

The old man stalled. How had they used the money in the past? The blind sister said they could all maybe just forget the debt and the old man put his foot down.

You'll pay me today, he said.

Whoever needs paying, explained the wheelchair-bound sister, *climbs into the tree and gets the payment themselves.*

She urged him on, said he could take a little more for his trouble. She took his wrist, led him toward the oak. The old man explained how he'd gone to such trouble for them, month after month, and now they were asking extra favors and expecting him to go climbing into a secret money tree in order to get paid for hauling all those supplies so many miles with his aching back and sore muscles and losing all the daylight to such a trip. But he climbed in, still complaining, and the large crack running the length of the tree's trunk just zipped up like the back of a dress, and they could hear him gargling the dead wood from outside as they made their way back to the house.

The circular wound on the blind sister's leg got worse in spite of the care they gave it, and eventually the sister in the wheelchair decided to cut the blind sister's right leg off to keep the infection from spreading. She held her sister's leg at the thigh and said,

Don't look. They both smiled, separately.

Who knows what they did with the leg? Buried it, fed it to the tree or themselves, maybe. After all, there was no longer a man to bring them fish and eggs. They didn't have a second wheelchair, so the blind—now one-legged—sister hobbled and crawled or rode in the lap of her older sister.

The wound from the amputation didn't heal well, and the blind, one-legged sister left streaks of blood in the hallways of the house, stains on her wheelchair-bound sister's lap. When they bathed together the water would cloud with blood. After only a short time, the wheelchair-bound sister was tired of all the mess and stink in the house. She thought of drowning her sister in the bath, but it seemed an unforgivable act. She went ahead with it, though, held her sister just under the surface and looked away. It took a very long time, but the wheelchair-bound sister dug a person-sized hole in the backyard and buried her dead, blind, one-legged sister near the roots of the tree that still held the old man she loved.

After that, she was totally alone. People say she wheeled herself out to the graves daily. They say she lowered herself from her wheelchair, sat on the ground with her hands behind her back, her fingers in the grass and dirt. They say she did this for years, would have done it forever, but her fingers spread into the ground behind her and took root. Her backside settled into the mud and her dress sank. Her body hardened until there was nothing left but a medium-size squat oak growing up beside the wheelchair. The two trees grew apart from one another for years until the old oak collapsed. The bodies made the soil rich, and the young oak flourished. So there's nothing out there now but an abandoned house and a healthy-looking oak beside an old wheelchair.

That's the story they tell, and with no better explanation at hand, we sit back and try to make ourselves comfortable. We listen for the parts that sound true.

In one story, the two sisters were Shel Silverstein and they wrote a book about a giving tree, which was the old man with whom they were both in love.

In the book, the old man was giving and kind and befriended a young boy, in whom both sisters saw themselves. The giving tree gave the boy everything he ever asked for, slowly disassembling itself as it did so. The boy was happy to come and ask and be given each and every thing—it felt like true love. He kept coming back and asking for more until there was nothing left and then he sat with the tree, who was the old man, and just waited for the next thing to happen—which they didn't know how to write, given it hadn't happened to either of them yet. The story was so touching it made both of them cry and their wife came in and said,

Shelly, what's wrong?

Nothing, Pet. Nothing, they said. *I'm just happy for you and Justin and feel fortunate for how well things are going right now with the illustrations and my poetry and I'm the kind of sad-happy that gets you crying after a couple of glasses of wine.*

You've had more than a couple, their wife said, and lifted the empty bottle before their moist eyes.

Maybe so, or a couple of big glasses, but what does it matter on a night like tonight? It matters very little if at all, that's what it matters.

The two sisters took their wife into their arms and she could smell the wine and whiskey and cod-liver oil on their breath and she started to wonder how much longer this kind of thing would go on, this kind of late-night, self-righteous drunken laboring over bizarre and upsetting kids' stuff and all the wild screaming fits and hurtful words they said to her, sober or drunk, it didn't matter. The two sisters began to dance with their wife and turn her back and forth and dip her down. They kissed her neck. They hummed and clicked their teeth and spun her again and the story sat on the desk, the decorative drops drying on its otherwise clean pages now worth so many millions.

The two sisters saw themselves in their wife too, though not as much so as in the boy.

Loosen up, they told her, and she went limp in their arms. They carried her to bed and set her down. She took the shape of a large stone.

In the morning the two sisters called their agent and said they had the new book. They drove Justin to school, and drove the manuscript to the agent, who presented it to the publisher.

This is supposed to be a kids' book, the publisher said. *It's too sad.*

The agent told them what the publisher said and they shook their heads.

No, no, sad is not bad. Sad is not something to hide from kids. This morning, for instance, we told Justin we were getting him a puppy and then we did not get him a puppy. The boy has to learn.

They could not help smiling at one another and the agent told them that was awful. The agent suggested they change the story so that the boy gave something back to the giving tree, something tangible. And they argued that he did, he gave the old man love, and the agent asked,

What old man? What old man, Shel?

They didn't answer because each was all of a sudden scared that the other would find out their true feelings for the old man, whom both of them loved very much and had based the tree on when writing the book.

We'll change the story somehow, they told the agent and he was satis-fied enough with their promise that they were able to leave it at that.

They went to the liquor store and bought more of the things they liked, ribbon candies and Red Hots, which they thought maybe Justin might like—if not now, eventually. They picked Justin up from school and told him he wasn't getting a puppy and he just stared out the window, as if to say, *I know, and you probably got more ribbon candy and Red Hots even though you know I don't like them*, which they had.

Later that night they tucked Justin into bed and he asked how their day was in that way-too-late kind of way that reads loud and clear as: *I just don't want to fall asleep quite yet*.
They sat beside Justin's bed and took turns telling him untrue stories about gnomes they'd seen and money they'd found and snails with giant eyes that told topical jokes and could fix bicycles.
When Justin was finally tired they went into their office and took out the manuscript from the night before. It wasn't much of a story, just a few words about a tree and a boy they saw themselves in. They liked the boy even though he was kind of a shithead. Their wife poked her head in.

Just checking.

They were planning to work late. Something in the story had to change. They needed to sell the thing and stop worrying so much about themselves in the story or the old man they were in love with. They didn't say anything about it, but they knew they would need to change a few things about the tree. Their wife would likely read the story and see something of the old man in their characterization of the tree, because who could really read this thing without noticing how very, very, very much they loved that tired old giving man.

In one story, the two sisters were an olive at the bottom of a dirty martini and were clipped in two by a set of large teeth.

One sister was the top half of the olive. She imagined herself in the mouth of the old man she was in love with. The other sister, the bottom half, was trapped under the tongue until she slipped out as the large mouth took the shape of laughter. There was something just right about the way she moved in his mouth and she knew he was probably thinking about it right then, whomever he was, and thinking about that made her think of the old man she was in love with, and how much easier it would be to keep the whole thing a secret, now that she and her sister were free of one another.

It was at the precise moment she was having these thoughts that the top half of the olive came sliding over the bridge of the large mouth's tongue and fell into her sister. The two of them were pushed back between the set of large teeth. The teeth came down and the sisters were mashed beyond recognition, swirled back and scattered on either side of the gums before the tongue twirled and grouped the bulk of them back in one place. Then they were swallowed.

They came apart as they moved down the throat of the man who wasn't the man they were in love with but who made them both think of the man they were in love with, and they came together again in a mucus-thick canal, which steadily drew them together toward the stomach. They cursed one another and wished more than anything that they were back in the jar where they'd been less than an hour ago, back when they were together and felt they could never be apart.

They reached the stomach and were digested. They were spread thinner than they could have imagined, but they found each other again. Rather they were forced back together, neither one knowing quite what to do with herself or what was happening, but both feeling resigned to this new torture that was their life.

They were forced together in a moist environment, and they settled there for a moment and rested. Things weren't perfect, but they were still. That was a place to start.

One turned toward the other suddenly, opened her mouth as if she were about to speak, but the water around them shifted and they were pressed closer together. The sisters, scattered as they were, thin as they were spread, started arguing for the first time in as long as they could remember. They argued and cursed but it did no good because the water around them only continued to be drawn away and they were only pressed closer together.

Then they were inched along. Slowly at first, and then with some speed. They were squeezed more tightly than if they'd been made entirely of the same material. After a moment of complete darkness they emerged into a great, bright space. They were flying, and then they sank.

Water held them, worked its way between them. They clung to one another then, but the water was relentless in its soft separation. They buoyed once, gasped for air, and were drawn suddenly downward by a spiraling current.

The whirlpool took them somewhere wonderful and strange beyond the capability of most to imagine. It was vast and dark and full of strange, sudden sounds. They looked to one another, but recognized hardly anything of the other's face. And yet what they found most shocking—other than the constant physical abuse, the unsettling shifts of their environment—was that they had each forgotten the man they'd been in love with. As they were slowly spread apart, melting away to only a trace of what had been, their thoughts drifted from this to that, but rarely to him. And when it finally came out, when one casually let his name fall at a moment when there was too little left of either of them to amount to any noticeable trace, neither seemed to pay it much mind. The name slipped out, and they dissolved until there was nothing left.

In one story, the two sisters took a tacit vow of silence.

They found their lives more comfortable in silence. It was peaceful. Things were good and they got by, until the older sister got sick. One afternoon, she fell and was unable to get up. From then on, she could barely sit up in bed. The younger sister called the doctor.

Hello, he said.

She said nothing, just stared ahead plaintively, and the doctor hung up.

She brought soup to her sister three times a day, made the bed one half at a time. When the younger sister tilted her, the older, sick sister's eyes had a sad look, but the younger sister had no way of knowing, really, if she was sad or not.

The two of them had always lived very private lives, and this was only intensified by the older sister's weakened state. The younger sister spent most of her time in the living room or outside, and came into her sister's room at regular intervals only to feed her, to bathe her, to change the sheets. In between these visits, the younger sister took to wandering in the woods behind their house. She didn't wander long, and never very far. She walked slowly, kept herself close to home. She walked out then circled back, and avoided using the same route when she could. For half a year, when she wasn't tending to her sister—doing the cooking, doing the cleaning, doing all of it—she explored that same small patch of land by different routes. The paths she walked, though winding and tangential, eventually wore impressions into the wooded earth. They traced snaking shapes around the trees, exposed roots here, a burrow there. An aerial view would have revealed something like an ant farm, labyrinthine meandering trails looping back toward one another, centered on the house. She stayed out longer in the evenings. The air was better at night, something about the cold. In the woods, she thought about her sister. She wondered what it was like to be bedridden, sick all the time. She seemed blank and appreciative. Was that what dying was like? Was she more and more indifferent to life, or was there a flurry of activity just beneath the flat surface of her face? The younger sister wandered her paths, running her fingertips along the trunks of the trees as she passed.

She had seen only one penis in her life. A man came to the house one day, claiming to be a traveling doctor out making house calls. He asked for a drink of water. He asked to come inside. The younger sister was only a teenager then and was excited to have an educated man come to visit. She showed him into the kitchen. Her older sister had gone into town for groceries. The younger sister thought to offer the man some toast and jam, but they were out of toast.

Would you like some jam? she asked.

He declined. She brought him the water and he thanked her.

He took the glass with one hand. The other was at his crotch. Before she knew it there was a curl of tan flesh ratcheting to life against the white of his dress pants. The newly revealed flesh was tanner than his hand, she remembered that. He held it at the base and moved his cupped hand along the shaft as if he were scattering birdseed. Her hand traced the curve of each tree as she turned around it. She couldn't remember when she left the house, how long she'd been wandering, but it was very dark. She turned back, followed a straight path toward the single light in her sister's window.

From outside the window, she looked in on her sister secretly for the first time, and caught her smiling. She was on her back in bed, a candle burning at the bedside. Her grin—lit and shining in the candlelight—looked cut into the flat flesh of her face. She lay there with the sheet at her neck, still and smiling, like a perfect jack-o-lantern. The younger sister was struck with the thought of kissing that strange mouth, of feeling it with her own. She knew the trees were to blame in some way. The bit of jam she cleaned off the floor with the hem of her skirt when the traveling doctor left later that afternoon. She entered the house, opened the door to her sick older sister's room, and discovered the face flat again, indifferent, gold in the light.

A doctor came to visit, the younger sister said, *and we fell in love. For six years now, we've been in love. I don't ever see him but I don't feel any different than I did the moment I laid eyes on him.*

The sick older sister did not budge. The breaking of their vow did not move her. The younger sister phoned the doctor again and asked if he made house calls. He said he didn't. Not many people did these days.

I love you, said the younger sister.

The doctor said nothing.

If not you, then one like you, said the younger sister.

Is this a joke? asked the doctor.

She hung up the phone, went back into her sick older sister's room, and made another vow of silence.

The older sister died a day later. The younger sister buried her in the backyard. After she dug the first hole and dropped in her sister, she dug more. She dug up some of the trees. She dug out most of the lawn, then most of her paths. She dug out the area around the plot where she'd placed her sister, and left the grave as a pillar in the center of an enormous trench. Digging got her nowhere. She started a journal. She was religious about it, wrote everything by candlelight. She passed each full page over the candle on her desk and onto a pile of pages on the shelf before her.

She might have kept these journals for months, weeks, years. It's hard to say. After the house burned down, once the remains were cool enough to dig through, only a few pages were recovered. And though the pages were full of writing, they didn't say much. At least, not much about what happened between the two sisters. It wasn't a journal, really, but they weren't stories. They could have gone on forever without coming to an end. She wrote the word *sister* a number of times. She wrote about the woods. She wrote the word *bird*. She wrote about jam and the hem of her dress. She wrote about a child. She mentions a clock. She longs for more light. She wrote *over the candle*. She wrote something else, and people have guessed it reads *hillock*, while others insist it says something altogether different.

In one story, the two sisters were Olympic swimmers.

More than that, they were transoceanic swimmers. They considered the Olympics training for their longer swims. One sister wore her medal as a point of pride. She swam with it around her neck on occasion. The other brought it home with her, but couldn't say what happened to it after that.

There was nothing they enjoyed more than exploring new water. At one point, at least in their minds, it became easier for them to swim than to walk. Walking was too abrupt and too restrictive. Swimming was an endless cycle of motion, as long as they kept it up.

It took months to swim an ocean, and they set out at least once every two years. They had a team that followed them everywhere, at a safe distance. The team paddled over—no running motors were allowed within half a mile of the two swimmers—and fed them, or buoyed them if they were training and had worn themselves out.

One morning, several days into a swim, an orca surfaced between the two sisters. It kept one eye on each. The creature maintained only a slow paddle to match their athletic-but-human pace. Both sisters were surprised, but neither stopped swimming. They slowed as the creature slowed, and soon it was hard to tell whether they were moving their bodies with their own casually pumping legs, or whether the steady ocean pulled them as it pleased.

Can you believe this? one sister asked, the weight of her silver medallion drawing her chin close to the water.

It's a baby, said her sister.

How do you know?

They listened to the creature's breath. They listened to the soft symphony of the water breaking against its slick body. Then it was gone. They looked for its shadow in the water beneath them, around them, but saw nothing. They kicked. They churned their arms. They swam, and thought less and less of the orca. Then it came back. It kept pace for a while, but at some point, it vanished. They swam until the sun set then turned on to their backs. Their team approached, placed the two sisters in their sleep harnesses. The sisters told their team about the orca and they all said,

Yeah? Neat.

Incredible.

Are you comfortable?

They had been at sea for nearly four days, but they had many days ahead of them. The youngest member of their team, a young man who hoped one day to swim the Pacific as well, asked if the orca was male or female. The sisters said they didn't know, and he watched them for a moment, as they floated, their arms by their sides at an acute angle. He wanted to ask something else, but couldn't think of anything. They were beautiful there. Two beautiful mermaids tethered to the edge of his boat. He ate a banana and watched them fall asleep. He thumbed the rope that held them both in tow.

Their bodies were trained to wake half an hour or so before the sunrise, and they were up and out of their harnesses before the young man had a chance to gather himself up and wish them a good morning. He watched them swim away, having eaten a handful each of powdered protein and chocolate. In the late afternoon, the orca surfaced between them. They swam on. The younger sister named it Clove. The older sister named it Orca.

Did you see your friend? the young man asked later that night, as they were clipping themselves into their harnesses.

They were too tired to give a real answer. They nodded, bobbed in the water. It had been a long day. It wasn't long before they were both fast asleep between the two boats that housed their team.

One boat contained all the food and a single woman, a writer, who had taken the job because she was in awe of these two women. She wanted to write a book about them. She didn't tell them, as she feared this would ruin the book. She chose the solo boat so she could write and think and talk to herself aloud about the secret book, without having to fear that anyone would find her out. The other boat housed the young man and the navigator. The young man was the doctor, a former EMT, and a quiet apprentice to the two women. The navigator was a much older man who spoke rarely, but was a complete professional. So professional, he even went by the name Navigator, and if it hadn't been for the paperwork filed before the journey, no one would have ever known his given name was Ashley.

Once everyone was asleep, the young man placed his small blue pillow over Ashley's face. He wasn't able to see Ashley's eyes pop open. He didn't see Ashley's tears at the realization of what was about to happen. He heard the muffled cries of Ashley's struggle, his legs thumping the back of the boat, the crack as he kicked the motor, the bubbling in his chest, and the sudden silence of his resignation. Ashley was still. The young man untied the other boat and let the writer drift out to sea. He paddled quietly. He paddled slowly. The two sisters were drawn along the dark surface of the water, and from a distance, they rippled wakes in the reflected light of a thin moon.

The young man paddled through the night with such diligence and care that the sisters slept on peacefully, dreaming of the next day's miles. They awoke half an hour before sunrise, by habit.

Every morning, when the two sisters began to move, their bodies would sink ever so slightly for a brief moment. The *splash*, they called it. It was their custom to let the splash take its course, to begin each morning with a dip into the ocean, their bodies and heads submerged, and to then rise up, unclip, and begin. That morning they rose, fumbled with their clips, tried to begin, but they met a tangled resistance. They sank. The harnesses were clipped and locked. Someone had threaded padlocks into the series of clips that held the sisters in their harnesses.

The sisters made a racket. They bobbed in the water. They flailed, kicked, yelled, and sank. The young man sat up in the boat. A few feet out were his two mermaids, flailing at the sight of the sunrise. It was morning and the other boat was nowhere in sight. He took a paddle out from its resting place on the side of the boat and began to paddle them in the direction that felt best. Maybe they would come upon an island. The two mermaids would be mad at first, but given the heroic nature of his love, their capture would appear less a kidnapping and more a kind of rescue. Out of the trappings of the water, after a lifetime of free island living, they would learn to love him back.

They tried to get the young man's attention. They called out for Navigator. No one answered. The young man paddled. The two sisters swam against the boat, and the young man paddled harder.

They swam. He paddled.

Their strength was enough to tow the boat on its own, but the young man's smooth strokes with the paddle proved difficult to overpower. However, the two sisters were set for endurance, and the young man's arms soon began to tire. He paddled on, the time between each stroke slowly increasing, and the two sisters swam at a steady pace. Eventually, he released. He collapsed in the boat. The two sisters swam on, feeling their victory in the slack that gathered beside them between each stroke. They swam for hours. The sun began to set. They swam until the sun was completely out of the sky and they swam on in darkness. They were brilliant swimmers, trained for the long pull, and they rode a wave of adrenaline from the foiled attempt at their capture. They were towing the man who had once been their captor, straight back to the authorities. They would have to start the swim all over again, and the frustration of that fact gave them even more strength to swim by. They swam and they swam. They had never pushed themselves this hard before. It was incredible. They watched the darkness set on the horizon before them. Their arms lagged. Their legs sank a little farther. The young man woke up, looked out, and smiled at his two mermaids exercising at the end of his rope. He set to paddling, and they were his again. This back-and-forth lasted the rest of the day, and by evening, everyone was starving. The young man hung his head between his knees. He no longer had any confidence, or took any pleasure, in his plan. It seemed likely they would die out there, or that he would go to prison.

He became determined to die out there, alongside his mermaids. He lay down in the boat. Birds circled overhead. His mermaids were swimming again, pulling him God knows where. He closed his eyes, and they swam on.

The next day, the orca came back. It surfaced between the swimmers, as usual.

Grab, said the older sister.

They each gripped a single fin on either side of the animal, and for a few moments, they slid along the surface of the ocean as if they'd been born there. But then the creature stopped. It looked at both quizzically, one eye on each. They weren't swimming. This was new, different. They were tired. They seemed sick.

Then came the shot. The fins went limp in their hands. The young man was slumped against the side of the boat, rifle at his cheek. The orca sank, buoyed back, then turned over, exposing its oily underside.

The three of them ate raw orca meat from over the edge of the boat.

I'm not such a bad guy, the young man explained. *I fell in love. The loneliness, the ocean, it all makes you crazy.*

The younger sister cried, couldn't bring herself to chew. Her older sister tore small pieces for her, and she swallowed the lumpy bits whole. Her older sister held each portion, like thick cottage cheese, at the front of her mouth, and sucked its juice through her teeth. The young man talked on and on. He didn't know what had come over him. This wasn't who he was. He was someone else altogether. He played baseball. He'd been a tutor. He thought he'd love the sea. He wanted to be like them. Ever since he'd read about them in the paper, he'd wanted to be just like them. He didn't know what had come over him. They ate the orca meat. They listened, but they didn't listen. It seemed an unlikely story.

In one story, the two sisters shared a keyhole.

It was undeniable, they decided, that there was something on the other side of the door. The door was locked, had been for as long as they could remember. It was made of thick wood, and neither of them had the strength to bring it down. So they kept watch. One sister got the morning hours. Her eyes were weaker and, when the light failed in the afternoons, she had trouble seeing. The better-sighted sister kept watch from noon until dark. But she often stayed up later, her eye affixed to the tiny shot of darkness there at the door. They were each confident they had seen something moving on the other side. One described it as a dark figure, hairless and shifting like a shadow. The other claimed to have seen what could only have been a man's hand.

No man could live in there for that long, the sorry-eyed sister said.

But what if he leaves while we're at the market, asked her sister. *Or at night? If he found times to leave, he could live in there for as long as we can live out here.*

The skeptical, better-sighted sister said,

We would hear him.

She watched for him, nonetheless. She woke up as early as she could, while her better-sighted sister was still asleep, tired from staring into the dark keyhole late into the night. The sorry-sighted sister would sneak to the keyhole and stare. One eye shut, one eye stuck to the cool frame of their unknown.

One morning she whispered into the hole.

If you're in there, she said, *you can come out. We won't hurt you.*

There was no response.

If you want, I can bring you food, she whispered. Then, *I think I'm in love with you.*

Nothing. She had trouble turning the keyhole over to her sister that afternoon. Some part of her was sure if she remained just a moment longer, he would say something back. But the rules were the rules, and neither wanted things to get nasty. They were eating less and less, each spending more and more time at the keyhole. The sorry-sighted sister woke at 3:30 each morning and saw the sunrise behind her in its illumination of the keyhole. First the gilded shape of the hole lit up, and then its shadowy contents. Somewhere inside there was a table … or a tall chair. There was a length of wood anyway. The floor shone, too. It must have been hardwood.

The better-sighted sister sometimes fell asleep with her face pressed to the keyhole. If the house shifted, her one eye shot open, surveying the darkness on the other side. She rarely fell back asleep.

Nearly five days passed, and neither sister left the house. They paced the kitchen, the perimeter of the living room, waiting for their turn at the door. The sorry-sighted sister still whispered. All morning, all the day through.

I imagine you're a kind man, she said. *I imagine you've got a good thing going in there and don't want to disturb us, and I appreciate that. We're happy and don't need any complications. But you've got us all tied up in knots out here. I'm not saying it's your fault, but your mystery has a kind of gravity to it. You could be the worst or the best man in the world; I'm in love with your shape.*

She ran her thin finger around the arc and the base of the keyhole. Nothing. The next morning she began by singing softly into the keyhole, a song about pigeons and cloth and ribbons wrapping around the shape of each new thing as it passes through to some holy space where maybe they could go and forget all of this, this whole mystery of waiting and darkness and burning eyes and lonely hearts. She was exhausted. She was hungry. Her better-sighted sister was asleep, leaning against the wall across from her. The keyhole was warm with the sorry-sighted sister's face. The wood of the door was soft against her cheek. A voice said,

Please.

She blinked.

Please, it said. *Go to sleep. Go to the market. You're killing me.*

The sorry-sighted sister looked behind her to make sure her better-sighted sister was still asleep. She was snoring softly, slumped chin to chest, her knees locked and her body still.

Open the door, she whispered. *I'll feed you. I'll give you water. Come out and see us. I knew you were there all along. It makes me very happy that you're talking to me finally and*—she was raising her voice and had to cut herself off before she woke her sister, who might scare the voice off.

Please, it said. *Life is very hard in here. You've got to understand.*

She did understand. She really did. Life was not easy for her, either. Her sister was very demanding, even cruel sometimes. They were alone most of the time. They didn't eat well; they never had. She didn't like hard work. She didn't like the walk to town. It was lonely and the people in town were complicated, and cruel, too. She did not like life outside the house and she did not like life inside the house. She liked the feelings that her thoughts about the keyhole gave her.

I've been waiting for you, she said.

Please, said the voice, *leave.*

Open the door, she said. *Open it and come out and let me see what I've been waiting for.*

I can't, said the voice.

Why? she asked.

She rattled the knob. She leaned away from the keyhole and rattled it again with both hands.

Please don't do this, said the voice.

Please don't do this, she said back.

She rattled the knob. She kicked the door at its base.

Come out.

Her sister's eyes opened.

Come out! The sorry-sighted sister was yelling now.

What's going on? asked her better-sighted sister.

The sorry-sighted sister left the room. She came back with the rusted axe they'd used for chopping wood nearly fifteen years before. With the strength of a madman she plunged the axe into the door.

You come out and I will feed you and give you your water.

She dug the axe out and plunged it again into the door's meat. Again, she plunged, using her whole body. Her hair came loose from its tie and whipped alongside the axe as she plunged it once again. And once more before the bulk of the door gave way and daylight from the open room shot out into the living room in a swathe of dusty beams. She let the axe fall. Her sister came to her side. Their hands came together, and they waited.

In one story, the two sisters decided to take a trip together.

They would fly to California to see the redwoods.

Some of them are thousands of years old, the younger sister had explained. *Imagine all they've lived through.*

She'd once met a man who told her about the redwoods. This was years before. She was on the porch, and he was passing by. He saw her from the road and came her way. He asked for water, maybe a bite to eat, and she gave him as much. He told her about the redwoods out in California and how old some of them were and she promised herself she would see them one day. After he left, she spent a good long while thinking about the redwoods. She imagined he went there when he pleased. He had that way about him, like he did what he pleased and nothing really got in his way except hunger and thirst and a little conversation. He might have been on his way to the redwoods that very day. He might have seen how excited she was when he started talking about them, and he didn't want to rub it in, that he was traveling and she was stuck on the porch, waiting for her older sister to come home with the soap and the pork belly. In the days that followed, the younger sister had pointed out the trees in the backyard, and talked about how lovely they were, how old and how interesting. She drew her older sister's attention to the liveliness of each curve of every branch.

There's a beautiful logic there, she explained. *To grow one way and the other—toward water, toward light. They're amazing creatures.*

They aren't creatures at all, said her sister. She broke loose a dead branch. *Food for the fire*, she said.

It started to rain. It rained through the night, rattling on the tin roof like an alarm. It rained for seven days without pause, showed no signs of stopping. The rivers rose and the earth was all mud.

In California there is sun all the time and it's never cold. In California you can see trees the size of mountains and the trees know things about the world human beings could never even dream. Some of those trees knew intimately species long gone. Some of those trees have lived longer than the men in the Bible, the younger sister explained.

A raindrop struck the pool in a tin can on the table, which had been set there to catch the leak. Another struck the older sister's arm.

So they decided to fly to California. They decided to dress up. Each chose an elegant hat with a veil, a small square of lace hung from the brim. The older sister wore blue. The younger, white. The sister in blue filled her purse to the brim with beef jerky.

Three hours is a long time, she said.

They waited in line at check–in, a single sack each, tied shut with a small rope. The airline employee took their sacks with a smile and the older sister, in blue, made a point to ask her younger sister, in white, if she'd caught the airport man laughing at their bags.

The younger sister, in white, said that no she hadn't, but she was sure they shouldn't be worried about that kind of thing right now. They were going to see the redwoods. It would be fantastic to see the redwoods so large and so old and wise with all they'd seen. She was convinced she would see the drifter there. She had a way of reading people, and the drifter would be back through those parts again, she had no doubt about it.

When her older sister asked why they couldn't sit beside one another on the plane, the younger sister explained cheerfully,

We bought the cheapest tickets we could find. We took the seats that were available. It's only three hours.

The older sister took a handful of jerky out of her pocket.

Here, she said, *you're going to need this. Three hours is a long way.*

From the airplane, the younger sister watched the hills go California. It was over before she knew it. The jerky remained in her pocket, untouched when they arrived. When they got off the plane the older sister complained about the bumps, that she was cramped, that she hadn't been able to get comfortable, let alone sleep. She was hungry and all her jerky was gone. The younger sister was too excited to think about jerky, or being tired, or how her legs felt. She looked for a cab. They had reservations at a bed-and-breakfast, but the younger sister wanted to head straight to the redwoods that afternoon.

With our sacks and everything? asked the older sister.

With our sacks and everything, her younger sister insisted.

I'm hungry, said the older sister.

There will be food near the redwoods, I'm sure of it.

The younger sister could have said anything, but none of it would have worked. Her older sister was tired, her hips hurt. She wanted to eat *real food.* So the younger sister would go by herself to see the redwoods, to see the man the redwoods made her think of, the drifter she'd only just met.

She and her older sister had traveled all day and, with the time it took to drop her older sister off at the bed and breakfast, it was nearly dark when the younger sister, in white, headed out for the redwoods. It was a forest, plain and simple. There were trails, but you could wander as well. The drifter wouldn't follow a trail, she knew that much. Not at the redwoods, which he knew so well. Being new to the area herself, she followed the trail's path, zigzagging between trees, cutting through the enormous ones that towered over her like the legs of a thousand-year-old giant. They were beautiful, too, not just magnificently large. They were a dusty brown, a coppery earth tone like she imagined canyons were at the bottom, or the earth between forests years and years and years ago. These trees had taken what was left of the color of the earth between forests and absorbed it into their bark to showcase the past like an amulet or a copper belt. She fell more and more in love with every tree she saw. She wandered for hours. It got dark. She hadn't seen the drifter but she felt more in love with him than ever, more in love with this place, which was everything she'd gone her whole life without thinking to imagine, and in which she was so perfectly capable of losing herself entirely.

The next day the older sister explained to the police that the last time she'd seen her younger sister, she was on her way to the redwoods, beef jerky in the small front pocket of her white dress. She spoke at an even pace to keep herself calm. She sounded calm. Her voice sounded calm. But she did not stop speaking, she hardly paused. She spoke on and on and repeated herself until she could think of something new to say.

She left yesterday. She was wearing all white. She was headed for the redwoods, but there's no telling if she made it there. She was wearing all white when she left. It was yesterday evening. She was heading out by herself because I was too tired to go and she wouldn't take no for an answer. She was dead set—I mean, she wouldn't budge. She couldn't wait. We don't travel much. This is our first time. We never do this kind of thing. So her not coming back, that means something happened. Nothing good could have happened. Can you understand that? She was wearing all white. There are coyotes around here, aren't there? Coyotes in the woods? They hunt in packs, right? At night? Oh God. She left last night. All in white. There are coyotes out there where she went. She had three hours' worth of jerky in her pocket.

There was a comprehensive search-and-rescue mission. They got volunteers from the town, policemen, even a helicopter. They searched the woods. They put up signs. They searched the canyons. Men and women formed a line and combed the woods and the desert looking for the sister in white. They never found her, though they searched for days. The children of the town were left behind during the search. Left with babysitters, left with one another. They might have put together a neighborhood game of hide-and-go-seek. They might have raided the cabinets of their respective homes. They might have gathered together, burned small household items together, sat around the fires and made up stories about the young woman together. Where she'd been going. Where she'd gone. What was left of her to find. When their parents came home after a long day of searching, the children might have told them these stories, and the parents might have listened. It's more than likely they were tired. It's more than likely they heard only the *sound* of their children's voices, excited or nervous or laughing and telling, and it might even have been a comforting sound.

In one story, the two sisters had a dozen children between them.

The children were from two different men—brothers. But it had been so long since the sisters had seen either brother, their memories of the two men had fused into one collective entity.

That man wouldn't raise a finger to stop the world from falling, one sister said.

He had five children, one to replace each of his senses, and the final one to take the place of his governing mind, the other agreed.

The sisters didn't care much for these children. One sister named each of her children Lyle, even the two girls. The other sister named each of her children after one of the apostles, but immediately after began referring to each as *that one.*

Tell that one to stop yelling at that one before that one wakes up and starts howling.

The sisters weren't hateful; they just weren't interested. They let the children run free most of the time, to explore the woods and streams around their small home. The twelve children learned to fend for themselves. They knew the surrounding area like a team of scouts. They created elaborate pulley systems and took a tree down with a few ropes, some sharp wood, and some scrap metal. Out of the tree they made chairs, a table and walls for a fort. They tangled the branches and made a decent roof. Every now and then, when it was warm enough, they were made to sleep outside, and so they'd built a home for themselves. The older set soon realized they would eat better if they hunted rather than relying on the gruelish meals their mothers prepared. So the children saved what food they were given and used it for bait. They ate rabbits, squirrels, birds, whatever they could catch.

One day the eldest Lyle discovered the uneaten carcass of an enormous blackbird. With his pinkie finger, he scooped the maggots from their canals. He plucked the feathers from the body, pinched ants from its sunken chest. He cooked the thing over a spit, half a mile or so from home. He offered bite after bite to the other Lyles as they watched. That one and that one watched him too, but none would eat the mess, even roasted.

That night, the eldest Lyle threw up in the living room. He threw up in the sink. The two sisters put him out back and he spent the night alone, sleeping on the porch right outside the door, alive with fever dreams and sweating a thick film along his arms and legs and chest. In the morning, they found him at the very top of an old oak tree. Nothing anyone said could get him down. The two sisters yelled, *Come down this instant!* and he squawked like a bird.

One of the Lyles threw a rock and hit the eldest Lyle in the leg. He moved farther up into the thinner branches of the tree. One sister scolded the rock thrower while the other cooed at the eldest Lyle,

Come down this instant, sweetie.

He did not come down. Finally, one of the middle Lyles stepped forward.

You best come down, he said. *You best come down because Mom didn't tell us the full story of that tree and I read the full story from one of the books on the shelf.*

None of the children had paid much attention to the single shelf of books installed above the family fireplace. The eldest children had shown no interest in reading or learning to read, and the younger children had followed in their footsteps.

Lyle continued,

And that tree is a haunted tree and we've been living our whole lives right next to it, climbing it without even sensing its being haunted. But it's a man-eater, they say. It will open itself up and swallow a man or a boy whole. Zip up its mouth like a set of blue jeans and the man or boy will drown in the aging wood.

The eldest Lyle shouted down,

Is that true?

The other Lyle nodded slowly, with assurance.

It is.

The eldest Lyle climbed down from the tree and asked what they had to eat. He'd thrown up the roasted bird all night and was sick all over and feeling weak. The two sisters took turns lecturing him and scolding him and reminding him how much trouble he'd put himself and the rest of them in and by the end he wasn't hungry anymore.

That same storytelling Lyle is now the town's own Lyle Garrity, soon-to-be mayor. And people whisper, as Lyle Garrity descends the stairs at the podium, wiping away sweat with a silk handkerchief, having laid them all bare with one of his mighty pre-elections speeches, they whisper,

He's got the gift, that one. He could talk a sick bird out of a tree and into being his own brother.

In one story, the two sisters had a set of relatively small wings, like those of a raven.

The wings were not strong enough to lift either sister, though both had tried at different times in their lives to fast to a point of near weightlessness. At eighty pounds, the older sister stood in the field behind their house and beat her birdlike wings for as long as she could. Feathers fell. She came in, worn out but unlifted. Not so much as a heel.

With time, they learned to ignore these wings as potential tools for flight. They saw the birds in their trees, or moving past in uninterrupted flight, and they looked away. They thought of something else. While they had once thought the wings were given to them for a reason—*we were selected; why us and no one else?*—they began to wonder whether it was a mistake of nature, a mutation, or actually a very common, but well-hidden secret. What good was a set of raggedy wings that served no purpose? They were a blemish, a burden, a set of dead arms.

One morning, hardly different from all the others, the younger sister decided to cook her wings into a stew and eat them. Times were tough and food was food. They'd eaten bird before, they weren't above it. It was a painful process, getting the wings off, but the pain went away once the saw was put back in the shed and she had begun depluming. There was very little meat on the wings, so they would mostly serve to flavor the dish. What flavor, she didn't know, couldn't say, but the wings were off and being put to good use, and that made her happy.

She stewed the wings for half a day then boiled down the broth. The older sister disapproved of her sister's self-mutilation, but stew was stew and shouldn't go to waste. It was a fine meal. The stew was sweet and tangy, with a hint of something like cinnamon. They thought of apple cider. They thought of pumpkin pie. It was uncomfortable at first, how much they enjoyed the taste. It seemed wrong. But it was something worth marveling at, the surprise effects of that strange ingredient. Both sisters savored the last few sips from their bowls and let their spoons come to rest still wishing for more. There was nothing left in the pot, nothing in either bowl. The older sister ran her finger along the inside of the bowl and asked,

Tell me again, how was it prepared?

The younger sister explained, all the while thinking, *We could do this once more. You know it, I know it. We have another set of wings sitting right here with us at the table. After that, we could go out looking for more. We'd be doing people a favor in a way, getting rid of the unnecessary things. Their clothes would fit better.*

The older sister offered to do the dishes. She offered to cook the meal the next night. But she did not offer her wings. They were flattened against her back by the heavy layers she wore. They twitched every so often, when she bent to pick up the bowls, the spoons, when she placed her hands on her hips and leaned back. The younger sister watched the wings shake like a set of ripe pears shifting in the breeze, ready to drop at any moment. Ready to burst.

The two sisters did not have much money and lived a very simple life. Their comforts were few, and their isolation was nearly complete. They went into town biweekly for food, supplies, to use the post, but they sought little in the way of entertainment or luxury. They had a small garden, but no fruit trees, no pumpkins. That's what the younger sister went to sleep thinking about: apples, pears, and pumpkins, simmering in cinnamon and candying in the pan. Her sister was a loud snorer, something she'd noticed as a child, but had learned to ignore. That night, though, each snore was like a stroke of the saw, steadily working that first pair of wings. The pain returned and she felt it in her shoulders, down her spine. She had sacrificed so much for the both of them, and her sister offered nothing in return.

She scratched, fingered the bandages stuffed into the moist pockets where the wings had been. The sisters were lucky to have the fortune of that fortifying flavor in their lives. That was something to be grateful for, something they could enjoy again, if only her sister would allow it. *Tell me again, how was it prepared.*

They say the younger sister sat on her older sister's back, pinned her down with her knees and the weight of her body, then clipped one wing with a set of hedge trimmers. When the older sister awoke, rattled by the pain and disoriented, the younger sister went in for the second wing but missed, accidentally plunged the trimmers between her sister's ribs. But some say the murder was in cold blood. Wings or no, she'd stabbed her with the hedge trimmers and left her in that old house like it was a tomb. People are still guessing at the reasons for doing a thing like that. They tell stories about the murderous sister still out on the hunt for fresh wings. Wings she's convinced are being hidden from her. They say she'll crawl through the window of a child's room and claw the child's back, searching for the spot where the wings will eventually break through. People say you can hear her scratching at the windows at night, looking for a way in, pressing her tongue to the glass. *She let her nails grow until they were tools. Her hair's gone wild. She's thin as a rake, holding out day after day for that smack of warm pumpkin, of spiced apple. The sound of the wind is her asking kindly, plaintively, for the treat. The scratching sound is her losing her patience. The shatter comes when it's already too late.*

In one story, the two sisters were reasonably well-behaved nuns.

They enjoyed badminton. They ate small amounts of cheese throughout the day. They read for hours each night, from the Bible, from the canon, occasionally from magazines, though Mother Superior frowned on it.

Their one weakness was for horseback riding. The feeling was like nothing else. Straddling that kind of power, they could canter, gallop, trot, jump, for hours.

One sister carried grain in the pocket of her habit. She fed the animals a handful whenever she passed. The other sister preferred to treat the horses to a good rubdown when she had the opportunity. Every so often, she'd have an hour or so away from her duties and she would go to the horses in their stable and rub one for a short period, until he shook with delight, trembled in her hands, and she would move on to the next horse with an air of accomplishment.

The two sisters didn't speak of their love for horses. If the subject of horses came up, they were more inclined to make a short trip to see the animals, and, if time allowed it, they would ride until they were all four worn out, spent and sore from the afternoon.

One day the horses took them farther than they had ever expected to go. They rode, their minds absorbed with pleasurable thoughts and the cool breeze of the afternoon passing around them, and before they knew it they were at a river. They had not known a river passed by the convent.

The horses approached the water and began to drink. The two sisters waited patiently, their heavy habits hanging from either side of the great animals like folds of skin. Just then, a young man appeared in the water. He was near the middle of the river, where the current was likely strongest. As he stood, water ran the length of his long black hair, down his shoulders and along the muscular knots of his back.

The two sisters watched him. They said nothing. The horses drank on, unconcerned.

The young man, dripping, solid, nude, exited the river and made his way to a small sack and a pile of wood they had failed to notice. The younger sister's horse flared his nostrils. He snorted, chuffed, lifted his head, and the young man looked over. He spotted the nuns and waved. He held his hand still in the air for a moment then vanished into the trees.

When the horses were done drinking, the two nuns had no choice but to head back to the convent. It was getting late and they did not know exactly how long the trip would take. On the way home, they talked about the young man.

He came out of the lake like a divine creature, the younger sister said.

That was a river, said her sister.

He came out of the river, then. He came out like he was made of the river or like the river had made him, like our lord made Adam.

It was a young boy swimming in a river, her sister explained. *It's likely he was a thief. Did you see that pile of wood and things, and how quickly he disappeared?*

That night, the younger sister lay awake in bed, thinking about the man and how easily he seemed to move in the current. *He must be very strong*, she thought. *He must know a lot about the river.*

By the morning, she was convinced she had to leave. In only one afternoon she had witnessed more strength and natural beauty than in all the years she had spent praying and eating and living at the convent. Until then, the power of the horse beneath her was the closest she'd come to this feeling. But now, with the river and the young man and the young man in the river and the pile of objects and the horses drinking and all the questions she had, she simply couldn't stay any longer.

She spent the day going about her duties, fully convinced she might leave at any moment. She didn't have a plan, exactly. She'd never given this kind of thing any thought before. She knew she'd bring a horse, knew in which direction she would ride—toward the sun, toward the river, toward the young man in the river with his things. She told her sister none of this, but her older sister was observant and noticed the change in her sister's behavior. She was less focused. She was daydreaming and careless in the preparation of breakfast and lunch. She watched the stable as if checking the clock. She smiled every so often, to herself, and finally the older sister, while they were digging in the garden one afternoon, tilling the earth, offered the following story:

Once, when you were very young, likely too young to remember, one of our sisters ran away. No one can say why exactly, she just left in the middle of the night. She left her things, brought no food, took a horse and vanished. As you well know there are miles of woods surrounding the convent in any direction, and only one town within a day's ride. Several of the sisters, concerned for her well being, put together a traveling party and rode to town together in order to find her and bring her home. But she had never reached the town. That same group of sisters then went back to the woods, they searched for their lost sister until they were out of daylight and they had to set up camp.

That night they claim to have been haunted. They heard voices in the trees, whispering, woods people talking. Something out there did not want them to remain. They felt the presence of the devil. None of them slept. They were awake all night, on watch, and they rode home at first light. Whatever it was in the woods that scared them, likely scared our lost sister as well. Scared her, or worse. She was never heard from again. Every so often, when the older sisters make trips into town, they ask after her, but no one knows anything. She simply vanished.

The younger sister daydreamed her way through most of the story. She agreed with her older sister, said that leaving the convent was a dangerous thing. Who knew what was out there? A young woman like herself could fall victim to any number of horrible creatures or situations.

That night she snuck into the stables and loosed one of the younger horses. He was not as well trained as the others, had been a burden since he was a colt, and the nuns were at a loss, really, for what to do with him. She placed a blanket across his back and used a stool to pull herself up and on. She'd packed a few days' worth of food and two books. The Bible and a *Reader's Digest* version of *The Count of Monte Cristo*, a book she had not read but knew involved a great escape. She rode out under the cover of night. Only one other nun saw her leave. A secretly superstitious sister, she was busy burying a potato underneath the full moon. The younger sister galloped by without noticing the potato-burying nun.

In the morning, that woman told the other nuns what she'd seen, the young nun riding off into the night on one of their youngest horses. The Mother Superior said there was little they could do but wait. If the sister wanted to leave, it was better they let her leave. No amount of convincing on their part would do any good if she had her mind set. They went about their daily duties. The young sister rode through the sunrise, deeper and deeper into the woods. She wasn't exactly sure where she was going; she just kicked her heels into the horse's side and rode on, hoping for the best.

They did not eventually come to the river. The horse brought her straight into town. In town there was a young man who was not the young man from the river, but he got in the way of her horse and startled the animal. She fell back, off the horse and onto the road.

I'm deeply sorry, said the young man. *I wasn't paying attention. I didn't see you, didn't see the horse.*

The horse had run a few feet from them and stopped. The young man helped the sister up and led her back to the horse, where they paused and watched one another, each waiting for the other to speak. The young man was very plain looking, but he had a kind face. She asked if he knew of anywhere in town that rented rooms for a reasonable price and he said he had an extra room where she could stay as long as she liked, and she accepted.

The room came with a small chest of drawers, a little table with a chair, a bed, and a lamp. She put her things away and sat on the bed and thought, *This will be a fine place to live for now, with this man, in this small house, with these small things.*

He knocked on the door and asked from outside if there was anything at all she might need. She was hungry, but didn't want to impose, so she said no thank you.

You must be hungry, he said, *after riding all day and never stopping to eat.*

He brought her a plate of greens and salted fish, which were foods she liked very much, and she let him sit beside her on the bed. They ate the fish and the greens together and after that he placed his hand on one of the folds of her habit. He did not know which part he was touching, but he held his hand there and watched her face light up. She did not say anything. He did not say anything. They stayed together in that bed and in the morning they went for a walk. They took long walks almost every day after that, and at night he brought her fish and vegetables and they slept together in that very small bed. She put her books in one of the drawers of the chest of drawers and never again opened that drawer for the duration of her stay with the young man. She was consumed with the activities of her daily life with the young man. He brought her a change of clothes and she tried them on, but did not like the way they looked. They were tight in certain areas, baggy in others. They were uncomfortable, inconsistent, and gave her body unexpected lumps. So she went on wearing the habit, with the rosary removed and hung from the bedpost.

One day, she was getting dressed in front of him at the beginning of the day— they were about to leave for their morning walk— and he caught her hand as she brought up the headpiece. She let her hair fall on the shoulders of her habit and gather there and they went out in the world like this together. She was falling in love with the man, so she decided to warn him.

I came here looking for a young man I've fallen in love with, she said.

He smiled. They were beside each other on the bed. The young man put his thin arm around her and tried to pull her close and she went on to describe the young man she'd fallen in love with as strong and brave and a kind of lone adventurer. The young man beside her kissed her neck, her cheeks, her shoulders.

And I must warn you, she said, *if I encounter him again, I feel my devotion to him will dictate my actions and I will go to him. My time with you has been perfect, but it is not why I'm here.*

He stopped kissing her, but stayed bent over at her side.

What are you saying? he asked.

She explained herself again, explained it was only a warning, she was not planning to leave anytime soon, but she wanted to be honest with him, it felt right to be honest. He went back to kissing her, and in the morning he left before sunrise.

She woke up ready for their morning walk, but he was nowhere to be found, so she put her hair up, put on the headpiece, the habit, and went outside to see if he'd begun the walk without her. She walked around the town most of the day and looked for him, asked after him, but she came up with nothing. She sat up that night, waiting for him, and he never came. Then she couldn't sleep. She was confident she heard the whisperings of wood people just outside her window. She was awake in bed for the entire night.

When the sun came up, she went downstairs. She waited there for a while. She cooked breakfast and watched the front door. She went outside, decided to walk into town again, to ask after him more aggressively. After that, she would ride out into the woods.

She toured the town asking after him and everyone answered no, they had not seen him, a little annoyed this time for the repetition. So she set out on the young horse.

She rode to the town's edge and into the woods. She did not yell for him, but looked after every movement with the keen fascination of a hawk. She saw birds. She saw squirrels. She saw several different types of mushrooms growing out of the center of a magnificently broken tree. An eruption of fungi spread from a crack down the tree's center and out, up toward the branches, down toward the roots. She went back to their home that night and tried to sleep there.

People do not just vanish, she told herself, but she could not stop thinking about the story her sister had told her. She grew suspicious of the woods, less so of her young man. *It's more likely,* she thought, *that he rode out into the woods and something happened to him.* The truth was, she did not know all the somethings he would or would not do. Their habits had been fairly simple. They slept together, walked together, ate together, walked together, wandered together, talked together and thought together and slept together. Where had this house come from? She didn't know. Where did the food come from? He bought it, but from where? She went to the store. She asked after him, looked for the items they ate with some regularity, salted fish, greens. She found the food and asked the clerk if she could have it. She would pay him back, she promised. He looked at her, at her clothing, her headpiece, and asked,

Where's your rosary?

She looked away.

I've forgotten it.

He gave her the food and she took it home and ate it on the bed. She would not be able to pay back the store clerk. He'd written a small IOU on a scrap of paper. He'd taken her address—the young man's address—and asked her name.

The debt was unsettling. She could not think of anything for very long without her mind turning to the impossible project of how to pay or work off this money owed. She blamed the young man for disappearing and not leaving her any means on which to live from day to day. She blamed herself for never thinking this could happen. At the convent, she had been able to work for her food. It was clear what to do and how to do it. But she did not want to go back to the convent. In the convent there weren't young men and long walks and salted fish and the weight of her thick red hair on her shoulders, or in a bun, or gathered like a horse's tail and tapping the back of her neck. She imagined the young men finding one another in the woods. She imagined them grappling with one another. She imagined them falling into one another, lunging for the final blow and landing together in a heap of muscle and bone and blood and all that passion for her and for the end of the fight. She imagined them dying together and a tree growing out of their bodies and mushrooms breaking out, splitting the tree down its center and scattering out into the woods around them. She imagined the small house full of people and everyone talking about what had happened, how exciting it was, how sad, how tragic and poetic and that that was what love was all about and she realized love was not a thing she understood and felt good about at all, but it was nonetheless something she felt for the two men who'd likely murdered themselves along with one another.

She took her books back out of the drawer and read what she could before her eyes got tired, alternating pages or paragraphs or phrases or passages until she began to fall asleep. *The Count of Monte Cristo* was more exciting than the Bible. But the Bible was very powerful, and as she read it she heard the voice of Mother Superior speaking the words aloud to her in her head. Neither book was very helpful, though. She brought them into the store the next morning and asked if they would work as payment for the food.

I will take them, said the clerk, *and allow the debt to remain a little while longer.*

He took the books. She left, without any food, still in debt, and still very much alone.

That night she led the horse into the house. He was shy at first, stepping on the stairs, lowering his elegant neck to pass through the doorway. She'd cleared the front room, removed the single table, the two chairs. She brought the sheets from her room into the front room and laid them out as a thin bed for the animal. He curled his front leg, tapped the wooden floor with the tip of his hoof. He bent his legs and curled into a sleeping position on the front room floor, which was something she had never seen him do before. She brought over her pillow, placed her hand on the animal's muscular leg. It was not like the young man's leg. It was not how she imagined the leg of the other young man either. It was a horse's leg. A magnificent, trembling, warm, horse's leg. The room felt tiny around them.

She slept and had a dream in which the young man entered the house. She opened her eyes. The horse stirred. The night was incredibly dark and there was nothing and no one there. The house settled beneath them. Somewhere, a window clicked. She ran her hand along the curve of the horse's belly and it rose, as if in protest, with an enormous breath. She lay awake, her hand still, until morning.

She brought the horse to the clerk and asked if this would cover the debt. The clerk agreed. She asked for a few more items to even things out. More food, some paper, thread and a needle. She took it all with her and set it on the table at home. It was every single little thing she had and hardly any of it would last for more than a few days.

She set out the next morning into the forest. She gathered her belongings. She brought the sheets too, in a small sack. She took the legs of the chairs from the front room. She walked all day until she came to the river. She had not known how to find it. She had not expected to find it. But there she was. She unloaded her pack.

She made a small tent from the sheets and the chair legs and a stray branch and she ate and watched the river and imagined the young man rising up out of the river, but he did not rise up out of the river. She wondered about her sister, the sisters, back at the convent. They were likely worried for her, or maybe they were proud. She had found her own way.

She became utterly devoted to the river. To its autonomy, its stability. She threw rocks into it, dipped her toes, and watched it move. But she must have left eventually. They never found the sheets. Only the holes where the chair legs had been, and a few dirty cans. They *did* worry about her at the convent, and for some time. Some of the sisters began to speculate on her misfortune, her extreme fortune, her newfound righteousness, her devolvement into sin.

She is having adventures, they said.

These are the most difficult trials of her life, said others.

Her older sister didn't speculate. She tended the garden. She watched the horses move, watched them breathe. She stayed up late and touched the horses and brushed their manes and thought of her sister, who was somewhere out there, along with their youngest horse, finding her own way. There was no need for stories. There was no such thing as adventures in this life. Not really. Only one thing, then the next. They lived on by the grace of God alone. Her sister lived on too, or she did not. The horses flicked their tails.

In one story, the two sisters found a bag of money in a ditch by the side of the road.

They had a short talk about it, and they decided to give the money back. But it was late, and they didn't have a car—otherwise they never would have found the money. The walk to town was very far, so they decided to wait until morning and keep the money with them overnight.

That evening, the older of the two sisters decided to stay awake all night, to watch the money while her sister slept. She sat awake, knitting and watching the money, and every so often she was overcome with the urge to touch the money, to check it, maybe count it, just to guarantee it was all still there. She lowered her knitting to her lap, rested the needles on her thigh, and stared at the bag.

Her younger sister was snoring in the other room. She had sleep apnea, so her snoring was terrible at times, but there were often long periods when she made no sound at all. While the older sister was knitting and listening and watching, whenever the younger sister's breathing paused, the older sister imagined her dead, and was happy. The need to watch the bag, to count the money, to stay up the whole night through, the pressure was all lifted, and she felt at peace.

She wasn't knitting anything in particular, just clicking the needles. She thought of all the things the money could buy. She needed none of it, but that didn't matter. Her life was good enough as it was, but money was money and there was no use in trying to pretend it didn't set her daydreaming.

She could populate the farm with actual animals, rather than the wild beasts that ran things now, broke into the house at night and ate up their apples and fish. She could buy goats and chickens and cows and dogs to chase the raccoons and birds and squirrels and snakes. Maybe a cat to catch the roaches.

A roach made its way across the wall, then toward the bag. It paused, seemed to take stock of the bag of money, and scurried toward it at a breakneck speed. She stabbed the roach clean through with the knitting needle, pinned the creature to the wall. She sat back in her chair and considered the insect as it thrashed its thread-like legs. She went into the bedroom she shared with her sister and stood beside her sister sleeping there. She brought the other knitting needle up to inspect its point. Her younger sister was suddenly awake and grabbing her sister at the wrist. Each sister pushed the needle toward the other until the frail elbow of the older one bent, gave in, and she plunged the knitting needle between her own ribs and into her left lung. She began to whimper, tears came, and she fell. Her younger sister took her in her arms and brought her to the living room. She laid her older sister on the floor, put her arms by her side.

Don't move, she said.

The needle was still impaled in the older sister's chest.

Don't move even an inch.

The older sister coughed, she couldn't help it. The younger sister shook her head. They didn't have a phone. The nearest town was miles away. The younger sister would have to walk for help, down the road alone, and the likelihood her sister would survive the wait was very slim.

Open the window, the older sister said, *I need air. It's hard to breathe.*

The younger sister opened the window and took a moment to look at the great oaks giving in the wind, at the sky full of stars like a bag full of money—at anything but her sister laid out on the floor with the needle in her chest. The bag was there, near her sister, open. The bills were out of their bands, loosely stacked and collapsing. The older sister had left them after counting and recounting so many times. The breeze from outside teased the mouth of the bag. Drifted the lip open, closed. The bills began to shift.

They say the moment the younger sister zipped the bag her older sister's soul left her body. One sister zipped the bag and the eyes of the other went flat. But maybe the money lifted up and out of the bag like so many flakes in a snowdrift. Maybe the power of the wind whirled those bills out and around them and the younger sister grabbed desperately at each one as it whipped past her while the older sister watched until she faded. Maybe she was thinking of all the happiness the money could have afforded the both of them. Or, if not happiness, all the time and freedom it would have provided, which they could fill with moments of happiness if they were so inclined. And maybe there was nothing malicious in the younger sister letting her older sister die that night. Maybe, for her, to catch the money was to save her sister. Maybe she imagined saving her sister's life with the money, or preserving the body in a special kind of mud. Mud that might fill the gaps in the tiny hole made by the ancestral knitting needle—it had been their mother's, her mother's before that—and would maybe jar the needle loose. Mud that would protect her. Mud that wouldn't age her. Mud that would keep her sane and still for years until long after the wound had healed and the younger sister had used the money to build a perfect life around them. Or maybe she imagined moving on. Burying her sister, selling the old house. Meeting a fine old man who would care for her and trust her. Maybe she imagined the kind of man who was good in so many ways, her sister couldn't have helped but fall in love with him too. Maybe those thoughts made her spiteful. Maybe there was no such man. Two bodies were found in a collapsed house, along with a bag of loose money. The town absorbed the funds.

In one story, the two sisters lived a long and uneventful life.

They were survived by thirteen children, Jose Garcia and wife Consuelo of Seguin, Rachel Alia of Seguin, Carmine Aylward and husband Dan of Hampton, MA, Maria Pina and husband Chilo of Seguin, Lupe Gonzalez and husband Felix of Seguin, Richard Garcia and wife Shade of Dallas, Alexis Garcia and husband Rosa of Seguin, Richard Goza of Houston, Estelle Martinez and husband Joseph of Seguin, Sylvia Goza of San Antonio, Elisa Gonzalez and husband Cain of Dallas, Patty Rodriguez and husband Ernesto of Seguin and Selena Castro and husband Angel of Seguin; thirty-two grandchildren; thirty-two great-grandchildren; five great-great-grandchildren; and sisters Adela Pina and Lupe Salazar both of Seguin. Honorary pallbearers are Richard Goza and Greg Putchi. Arrangements by Gloss Funeral Home.

In one story, the two sisters purchased a computer.

They had one working power outlet in the house, occupied by the lamp and the heater. It was the middle of winter, and that heater wasn't going anywhere. They decided to get rid of the lamp and use the light from the computer screen in the evenings, as needed. They would do all of their nighttime work—eating, reading, knitting, clipping, mending odds and ends—by computer light.

It looks like a ghost, one sister said.

From the hallway, she pointed toward the living room where the crackling blue of the undying monitor held a dome of eerie light against the wall.

It's a computer, said her sister.

She went to bed. The other sister turned toward her door, but turned back around once her sister disappeared into her room. She sat down in the hallway to watch the light. It wasn't frightening, or altogether that strange. She was attracted to it. She thought of ghosts. The indeterminate nature of ghosts. She'd seen a ghost once before.

Late one night, she was pacing in the living room, unable to sleep, and the ghost of Davy Crockett had floated right through their living room and on through the house. She watched him until he disappeared. He didn't seem to notice her. He just passed by, the tail of his coonskin hat bouncing as he went. She had woken her sister up and told her the story.

Go to bed, her sister had said. *There's no such thing as ghosts.*

The ghost-seeing sister was never fully convinced that she hadn't seen what she saw. She'd seen Davy Crockett. So she'd wondered about ghosts from then on. Wondered how they thought of themselves, if they had ghost quests on which to embark, if they even knew they were dead. To be able to travel through walls like that, from room to room, Crockett had to have noticed something was different. Something was not like before. Or could he not remember before? He certainly had an air of purpose about him as he passed. He didn't slow down. He didn't take a look around. But then again, maybe he had been there for some time. She didn't know. She'd been occupied with these thoughts for months after the sighting, and every once in a while in the years that followed. They're what occupied her as she sat there in the hallway, watching that computer glow. Thoughts about ghosts and what they knew of what they were doing. Thoughts about Davy Crockett. Thoughts about that relentless shade of blue radiating from the living room.

The older sister came to know all of this of course because the younger sister put it all in the mess of a suicide note she'd left open on the computer's desktop. It was in part of the note, at least. The only part dealing with death. The only part offering any kind of explanation of the act—this preoccupation with the lives of ghosts.

That Davy Crockett was a handsome man, the older sister would tell people, often uncomfortably close to a comment or exchange about her younger sister's untimely death. *He was one of the few men you could count on, a real life hero, they say, even though you can't believe everything they say, no, but you can be sure they say it for a reason,* she said.

After the suicide there was a slight but noticeable rise in local sales of Davy Crockett biographies. In all but two of the popular titles, he is championed as a hero. In one, the least flattering depiction of Crockett occurs in a passage that takes place after the Battle of the Alamo:

Ex-Congressman Davy Crockett was one of the few survivors, discovered well into the pillaging of the great fort, curled and weeping beneath one of three raised beds, which were provided to the most prestigious members of the resistance. He was chewing his trademark cap, bathed in his own urine.

The other book holds records of variations on the number of myths told by, or spread about, Mr. Crockett. It states:

Of the many stories told about Congressman Crockett, including those told by himself, the most unlikely is that of having, at the age of three and with no adult assistance, killed a bear alone in the woods. What speaks to Crockett's storytelling, and to the resultant success of his mythologizing, are the number of recorded repetitions of, and variations on this tale, and others like it, as well as this quote from Daniel Boone, 'If you had heard that story yourself, from his mouth, you would never have once doubted that that three-year-old did indeed throttle that bear through until its very last breath. There is no doubt in my mind. I'm thinking of it right now, and few things have ever turned out feeling this kind of true.

In one story, the two sisters were a child who would not grow old.

The parents stood over the mat where the child slept, watched the child, whispered a kind of concern, but were really more charmed by the small creature than anything else. The child was soft and underdeveloped in all the best places. Everything about the child was smooth and tiny and wriggling. Friends came over for dinner and said,

She's so delicate. By which they meant: *small for her age. Tiny, really.*

The parents took her to a specialist.

What do we do? the parents asked.

She's two, he said, *until she's three, until she's thirteen, I suppose.*

The parents took the child to a second specialist, a developmental specialist.

She is a perfectly cogent two-and-a-half-year-old, said the second specialist.

But we had her three-and-a-half years ago, said the mother.

The second specialist said,

She is a perfectly cogent two-and-a-half-year-old.

The parents abandoned the project of seeing specialists and went about raising the child who would not grow old to the best of their ability. They often took the child to see a large tree in a park near their house. The tree had thick branches that reached over and all the way to the ground and the child was able to climb on them and pull at them while the parents watched from a nearby bench.

They developed a routine, learned to anticipate the child's moods, wants, needs. There were advantages to having a perpetual two-year-old. The parents read the same bedtime stories, over and over. The child learned but she did not learn. Her vocabulary grew, but her worldview was capricious and unsettled. She spoke all the time, repeated herself often. She was potty trained, but still had accidents. She used a fork and knife, but managed only very small bites. The parents were even able to get to sleep early every so often. On these nights they would say things like, *We've got a good thing going*, their six-year-old–two-year-old silent in the next room.

One night they ate dinner at a Mexican restaurant. There was a bowl of chips in the center of the table and the child worked a single chip, piece by piece, with her hands, her gums, her lips, her small teeth. The parents sat across from one another and talked about different things. The child repeated some of the things in between mouthfuls of chip.

I need new boots, she said.

Her parents acknowledged her when she spoke, with a reply or a gesture or a question, and they went on talking.

Sit down in your chair, the father said.

I am, said the child, but they did not recognize the voice. She was nearly eye level with them now. She reached over, plucked a chip from the basket, and submerged it in the small dish of salsa. She ate the chip whole. Her parents watched in silence. Her clothes were tight to her body, swollen at the seams. There was hair on her arms, her legs. Crumbs gathered in her beard. She watched the both of them, bleary-eyed. The child cursed at them in what might have been Russian. She took a handful of chips. She ordered a shot of tequila, then another upon its delivery. The parents divided up their burritos.

I need new boots, the child said in a heavy accent.

You'll need a new shirt too, sweetie. The mother gestured at the ribbons of cotton at the child's shoulders, on the floor near the chair. The child ordered a third shot and asked the waiter where the "buckle bunnies" were.

Later that night, the mother tucked the child into bed. They had carried the child into the house. Her body hung heavy on each step and she'd barely made it out of the car before throwing up somewhere in the darkness of their unlit lawn. The mother wiped the child's mouth with her sleeve. She tucked the edges of the blanket around the hulking mass. The father joined her in the doorway and they watched the body heave and begin to snore.

There has never been an easy part to this, said the father.

There was at least one easy part, said the mother.

Their child slept on as they probed and pinched and kissed in the hallway outside her bedroom door.

In the morning, the child didn't say much. She asked for eggs but ate only a bite before pushing the plate away and hanging her head. She asked for Tylenol, for water.

Your mother and I think you're ready to start school, said her father.

Okay, yeah. I know, said the child.

A local public school ran from kindergarten through middle school, and was associated with an adjacent high school.

Give it a few weeks, said the father. *We'll see where you fit in.*

The child said nothing.

On the first day of the semester, they introduced the child as their daughter. She wore her dad's shirt, his sweatpants, an old sweater.

The principal of the high school called them that afternoon and said the parents had to pick the child up. She was no longer welcome.

Why, asked the father, *has she performed badly?*

No, said the principal, *she's light-years ahead of most of the students, actually. She's a whiz at math, physics, nearly everything we threw at her. A real bright star. But she's a bully*, the woman explained. *She tried to force another kid into letting her give him a tattoo with a needle and a ballpoint pen*, she said.

The Mickey Mouse is very important, their daughter later said.

She sat behind the kitchen table, her two parents across from her, arms at their hips, shaking their heads.

It is a sign of power and of money and of security and of strength and many other good things. I was not doing a wrong thing because the child wanted me to, you see?

Don't do this to us, said the father. *Do not do this.*

He looked all around the room before his gaze finally settled on the mother. She shook her head, her eyes wet.

What happened to our little baby forever? You were going to be our little baby and what happened?

The daughter spat into a glass on the table, blew her nose onto the floor. She shrugged and the lights in the room flickered.

I can fix the wiring, she said, *if it's a problem with the wiring. Would that make you happy? If I fixed it?*

In one story, the two sisters were bound and gagged and put in the trunk.

When they came to, saltwater poured over their heads and someone shouted in an indistinct tongue. They were blindfolded with a rag, and all around them was the hum of activity. Telephones warbled. Bus brakes released. They were outside somewhere. They could feel the breeze. The voice went on, as if it were counting. This . . . then this . . . then this. They struggled, were unable to move. They were doused again with saltwater. It soaked into the rag and stung their eyes. They did not know what they had done. They had done nothing. They were silent. A car faded past them. They struggled to speak. They tasted iron and fabric softener. They heard a family pass by, two distinct children's voices, a mother saying no . . . no . . . because . . . no. They heard the rattle of buildings and the clang of used scaffolding. They were outside somewhere, in what sounded like a city. More saltwater.

One sister imagined a bagel. Her fingertips were in the image as well, dangling a sliver of lox above the uninterrupted swell of cream cheese. She wanted to shake her head, to shake the image from her thoughts, but her neck was sore and would not act as quickly as she would have liked. Instead, her head just sagged, bounced up, sagged again. Something was biting their knees. The sound of a pedicab bell dinged. How could no one do anything?

They heard the sound of collective anxiety. They heard the sound of a knife, or a comb, pulled from a denim pocket. They trembled in their bindings, but it hardly showed. There were birds all around them, some distance up. They made a din like it was cloudy out. One sister urinated. The air was thick with that smell, then the smell of a lake. The breeze changed directions. Their captors were still yelling, taking turns. They were explaining something. This . . . or this . . . then this. There was the prolonged metallic ringing of a large rubber ball smacking its way down a flight of stairs. There was the sound of someone sipping. One sister imagined grease on a pan, sizzling, popping, arcing spots of scalding oil out into the room. She imagined her thin arm dodging the oil, then her hand turning down the stove. Something was biting her calf, her thigh. She tried to talk, but still couldn't. Saltwater poured over their heads once again and when the two sisters came to, they were in a field. They were not bound. They were not sore. They were in low, scratchy grass. Their arms were streaked with dirt, their faces too. Their hair was wet. They rose from the grass at nearly the same time. They could speak again, but could not understand what the other was saying, or what exactly was happening to them. They wanted to walk home, but did not know the direction. They walked in one direction, toward the sun. One said that this way the day would last longer. It could have been a dream, the saltwater, the sounds from the street. When they spoke, the words went out and settled separately. The sound settled in the grass, sank toward the horizon, faded like the sound of a car passing or the ding of a pedicab bell. They met a road. They turned right. A car passed and they waved it down.

We don't know how we got here, they said. *We don't know where we are.*

The driver asked where they were headed, at least.

Home, they said.

He offered to drive them there. He fed them jerky from his glove compartment. He played country music on warped tapes and sang along. Every now and then he would stop to talk about the lyrics.

What he's saying here is that a man can be two things. More than two things, I'd like to think, but he's saying a man can be two. The man he wants to be or the man he hates. We're both at the same time, or have the likelihood of being either. He's saying man, *but I think it could be anyone really. A boy, a girl, a woman. People can and will be anything it's in them to be, at least for a little while, at least at some point.*

The country songs played on.

*She's saying here that a bar ain't no kind of bed, which I think goes with-
out saying . . . but she's singing it all new, as if the thought had never crossed
anyone's mind. I like the idea that that's why I like music.*

The sisters didn't say anything. The driver was friendly, talk-
ative, happy to have company, it seemed. They were happy to feel safe.
Happy to feel the AC on their arms. They felt less like they had been
lying in the grass, less covered in dirt. Their hair was drying, starting
to curl up.

The driver liked poker. He had all kinds of strategies for it, but
he still lost a lot of money to the habit. He smoked, offered them
cigarettes. They said,

No thank you.

They turned onto their road and recognized a neighbor's house.
The ditch along the side of the road like a canal. The gravel from
adjacent gravel roads, spilling onto the paved road like dust. They
changed their minds.

Take us to the police station, they asked, and he was more than
happy to.

It was more time to talk. More time to sing along with these
sad country songs and talk to the nice women on a beautiful day. He
turned the car around.

*This song I don't like much. There's something mean about it. I've got
some ex-wives, three to be honest, and you can't go on hating them forever.
You can't blame what's happening to you on them. You get rained on once,
that's no one's fault really, maybe. Three times, well, you should have worn
a jacket. You should have thought things through a little more, maybe. Rain
will wear away a mountain, for Christ's sake. But now I'm just rambling on.
I apologize for it.*

He turned the radio up for the song he did not like. He stayed with them at the police station while they gave their report. They told the police everything that's been recorded here. The police took the driver in for questioning. They read him the two sisters' statement and he was alarmed and confused, but he nodded along to his own words as if they were a familiar song.

The police looked into the kidnapping for over a year and came up with nothing. They re-read the statements over and over again. They brought the sisters back in for more questioning. Their memory of the event was less and less helpful, more and more indistinct. The story of their release and rescue was the least consistent or believable. They spoke less and less about what they did not remember: where they had been, how they had gotten there, what, exactly, had even happened to them. They spoke more and more about the driver: he had appeared from nowhere, he was a stranger, he cared about them deeply, he seemed like a drifter, he had rough hands. They had opened their eyes, and there they were, beside him in the cab of his truck. And he was grinning at them. Grinning and telling them about all the things a man could be. After nearly a year, the police arrested the driver. In his truck, they found two bags of road salt, a cooking stove, bacon, bagels, and a small bell. He was tried, convicted of kidnapping and attempted murder, sentenced to sixteen years.

In one story, the two sisters met in high school.

One was a senior, the other a freshman. For whatever reason, they were drawn to one another. The senior was excited each day to see the freshman, even only in passing. The freshman was a little less sure of things. She liked the attention, but was inexperienced and cautious. Eventually they agreed to go to a movie together. The senior was very polite. She picked up the freshman, held her door for her, paid for the tickets, the refreshments, the candies, etc. She brought her home after the movie without making any moves or coming up with any reason to prolong the date, to keep the freshman in the car a little longer. Even the freshman's parents were surprised to see her home so early.

You screw it up? her father asked.

She didn't say anything and went straight to bed, but not to sleep. She was awake for a while, thinking about the movie and what she might have done wrong. Why hadn't the senior made a pass? She thought about it late into the night, until she couldn't think that well anymore and fell asleep and dreamed confusing dreams about the senior and the cartoon characters from the movie.

When she woke up the next morning she realized what had gone wrong. They had seen a cartoon, and there was nothing sexy about cartoons. At least not that cartoon. So that day at school she proposed they go exploring together that weekend. The senior agreed to the idea, let the freshman choose the area they would explore.

It will be fun, the freshman said.

She tried to sound enticing, but she was too cold or something because she shivered as she said it, and to her she sounded afraid.

That weekend they explored the quarry on the outside of town. It was basically a giant hole with a spiraling path leading down to a pool at the base. It was a crater, a man-made lake. When construction projects in the town dried up, things at the quarry slowed down, and all the hollow places filled with water.

The senior was having cramps that night and she complained about them the whole time as they spiraled downward toward the pool.

Ow, she said. *It's from these iron pills. My mom makes me take them because my hemoglobin's low. Ow. Or she thinks it is, because I keep fainting.*

The freshman tried to sound sexy,

Yeah?

These weren't conversations she'd had before, not with people she wanted to seem sexy to, and she had only recently found herself wanting to seem sexy to anyone. And why did she need so bad to seem sexy to this senior? She wasn't sure, but it felt right to try. So she tried.

How do you take them? she asked. *Do you swallow them? Put them in your food? Crush them up and sprinkle them down the length of a banana?*

Ow, the senior said.

When they reached the water, the senior sat down, doubled over and held her stomach.

Do you want to swim? asked the freshman.

No, ow.

The senior didn't want to walk back up the spiraling path either. So they sat by the water in the quarry and the freshman talked. At first she asked questions, but received only monosyllabic answers—*Yes, No,*

Ow—so she spread the questions out more and more until she was just talking and talking. It was nice to talk and talk like that, no one interrupting. No concerns about tossing the ball back and forth. She could just go, and the senior was either listening or not. It didn't really matter. She told her about her parents, about her dad. He was very clean and often mean. He made her want to smash light bulbs. Her mother was understanding but confused. Her mind was slipping, maybe. Or she chose not to listen most of the time, to pretend she didn't understand what was maybe too much for her to think about. Her daughter as a person, an adult, for example. The freshman couldn't explain it exactly. Her mother talked like a baby sometimes, goo-goo-ga-ga, kinds of things. To her father, to her. It was maybe supposed to sound affectionate, but it just sounded awful.

Ow, said the senior.

The next morning the freshman was more excited than ever to see the senior. She watched down each and every hallway. She thought she saw her a number of times, but it was never her. The freshman still had so much to say, so many thoughts to finish, or refine. So much of what she said had just come out, she wanted to tweak a few things, soften something in the word choice. Some of it didn't sound right when she said it back to herself later that night, relishing the flavor of those hours at the quarry. She had been up most of the night, revising. But she hadn't seen the senior all day.

Around lunchtime she got nervous. The senior usually took her lunch by the choir room, propped up against the trophy case, using the back of her bag like a TV tray. The freshman had sat with her once, and they ate and listened to the choirgirls sing. There was something inviting about it. Something inviting, even, in the breaks, in the pauses when the choirmaster interrupted, instructed, recommended. The sounds were indecipherable and the two of them had sat outside the door, silent, listening like you would to a lake. That was before the quarry, though. Before the rush of words and stories and thoughts she'd never thought to have, would never have otherwise said, and now she couldn't imagine sitting outside that choir room door for that whole long forty-five minutes without so much as saying a word.

It would be unbearable. Like the day was turning out to be. Because where was she? Where was this senior who had been such a good listener the night before and . . . then she thought, *What if something's really wrong? What if it wasn't the iron pills? What if she was very sick, or dying? There were these cysts girls got on their ovaries, her sister had them, and they were really uncomfortable and awful for her sister and what if the senior had those? What if something happened to her after they left the quarry? After they went their separate ways? What if she was wrestled to the ground by a set of thick arms and dragged somewhere and left somewhere and what if she never came back? Could never come back?*

The freshman sat outside the choir room door listening to the singing, dreaming up all the awful things that were keeping the senior away from her regular lunch spot. *Their* regular lunch spot.

She might have dreamt forever about what had happened, but she chose to dye her hair instead. She dyed it black.

This is for her, she said.

She got a tattoo, a small cartoon bird on her side, right at the bottom rib. It looked lonely. She got a second tattoo. A second bird kissing the first bird. Weeks passed. She got her navel pierced, her eyebrow. Her parents started asking if something was wrong. They didn't know about the tattoos. They didn't like the eyebrow piercing.

It looked more interesting before, her father said.

She slammed the door. She started slamming doors. She left school when she felt like it. What was the point? Who was it saving? It wasn't saving anyone. Where was the senior? The freshman went to a museum. She wandered from room to room, but didn't really look at the things. Everything was there to teach her something, but she couldn't tell what exactly.

On the way home from the museum, she stopped at a small gallery. There was a room marked off by a velvet cloth. She went in and sat down on a box bench. She crossed her legs but the chains that ran from leg to leg snagged, and she had to uncross them, untangle the mess and try again. While she was doing this she heard a voice say,

He took me to the bunker and did what he wanted to me and I didn't say anything. He asked me if I wanted food. I said I didn't. I thought I could prove something by not eating. He didn't make me eat. After a while I started saying, yeah, please. And he fed me. He brought me things he'd cooked himself. He told me I was his girlfriend. At first I didn't say anything because I didn't want to say no and get hurt more. He raped me a few times per day for several weeks. Or that's what they say. I wasn't sure how many days had passed when I was there. He didn't have a schedule to when he came and went. It was dark when he wasn't there. He told me I was his girlfriend and I didn't want to say anything. I don't remember when, but I started saying thank you. When he fed me, I said thank you. When he left, I said thank you. Then, he told me I was his girlfriend and I said thank you. I don't know why I said it. I wasn't thinking clearly. It made him happy though. I think it made him happy. I think he thought he was being nice to me. Nice as he could be given the circumstances.

The freshman was transfixed. There was no face, only a voice. The room was dark but for a fading gray square that lit the top right corner of the wall opposite her. Every now and then, glitter appeared on the gray. It looked random. The gray was dull . . . then the glitter struck, lit the gray like a stroke of lightning and it made her shift in her seat. The voice continued, listing things that had happened. What she did during the day:

I chewed my cheek sometimes. Other times, I screamed for help. Other times, I sang.

The freshman listened carefully. Was it her voice? The senior's voice? How did she know it? It seemed to change a little each time; between each pause, something shifted. She didn't know how to describe it.

One day the police came. I was scared of them at first. They asked me if he was there and I said no. They asked if he did certain things to me. I said yes to all of it.

It sounded like the same woman, growing older with each new phrase or word. It was awful. She wanted to show it to someone. She wanted to get it tattooed on her chest. On her ribcage. She wanted it tattooed through her chest and onto her rib cage. Then she would show someone the tattoo. It was sad in that space, she was even crying. It was a sad story. She felt more sure of things, of herself, of herself in the world. It wasn't a good feeling or a bad feeling. It was a firm feeling. She was happy people made things out of things, and she wanted someone to sit beside her right then, so she could tell them about the idea she had for the tattoo. She didn't like dating anymore. She got more tattoos. None of them were right.

GAINESVILLE

It would be an exciting thing to see, all the cut trees stacked back and forth, and piled up toward the sky where there was only more space for them to be stacked higher. The boy, Sonny, took an axe to the first and looked around him thinking how easy it would be to just keep going, to axe this one then that one and never to stop until all the trees were brought down and stacked and his arms were as big as cannons. He axed again and was a little more tired this time, but he thought of the cannons his arms would be and swung once more into the meat of the tree.

The axe stuck in the center of the trunk, so he had to pull just about as hard as he'd swung in order to remove the axe, and then he had to swing it again.

"If you stack them high enough," his brother said, "we can climb them and grip onto the edge of those rain clouds there and maybe slide over into the center of them."

Sonny knew his brother was probably lying, but he swung anyway. The idea was exciting.

Sonny's brother was sprawled out on the patio furniture, propped low in one swivel chair, with each extended leg rested on one of the two chairs in front of him. He was surrounded by beer bottles—some empty, some full. They were all warm.

Sonny's brother's friend, Rissa, was in the grass nearby. Sonny swung and looked back at Rissa and she pulled the grass out of the ground and stuck it in her shirt and Sonny thought about how great it would be if he were that grass sliding down and getting stuck.

Later they were all in the house and the axe was outside, leaned against the tree that was all marked up but still standing. They were watching TV, some show about teenagers trying things out, and Sonny asked Rissa if he could see where the grass had gone. She hit him in the mouth and told his brother and his brother hit him in the mouth a few times more and told him to get out so they could finish watching their show without the little pervert getting all worked up.

Sonny wandered around the house a few times before taking off down the road to the neighbor's house. He knocked on the door and the frog girl's mom answered and Sonny asked if Nicole was home and her mom went and got the frog girl. They called her the frog girl because her neck was as thick as her head and she gargled sometimes and spat, which they said was just like a frog, though it wasn't exactly.

The frog girl walked to the park with him, went on the swings with him, told him she liked the things he talked about—like cars and bicycles and his brother and his girlfriend—even though she didn't seem to be listening. Sonny got her to climb under the jungle gym by saying he'd found money there and when she was bent over, looking for the money, Sonny put his hand up her skirt and she started yelling and ran home to her mom, who definitely called Sonny's parents, so Sonny was scared to go home.

He walked a mile to the grocery store instead, and pocketed a handful of beef jerky sticks and a beer from a six-pack and tried to walk out with them, but the manager stopped him by tapping one shoulder and moving to the other side, so as to trick him. Sonny started to run, but the manager was faster. He got in between Sonny and the door.

"Call the police," said the manager, and Sonny started crying because the day had started out so well and all of a sudden it was the worst day ever. "Call the police," said the manager, "I've got him."

The police came and they arrested Sonny for stealing a beer and a handful of beef jerky sticks, and they brought him home to his parents, who were upset with him already, but were heartbroken and full of rage at the sight of him being unloaded from the police car.

Sonny's parents didn't know exactly how to handle a thing like this. Neither of them had misbehaved when growing up, not really, and they'd never gone beyond a grounding with Sonny's brother. But something severe had to happen, so Sonny's father took the boy into the living room and told him to drop his pants.

"My what?" Sonny said.

"Your pants and your underwear."

Sonny was convinced his father was joking until the man got irritated and tugged the boy's shorts down himself. Sonny started crying then and his father hit him a few times on the exposed skin, but the act didn't feel right, it only felt like a sloppy way of handling things, so he stopped after a few strikes. Sonny was sobbing and fell from his father's knee and just cried there in the middle of the room while the whole family watched and wondered what all of this might do. It didn't seem like it would do any good at all. Sonny's brother was happy to see the boy in trouble, but didn't much like the sight of him crying and squirming in the middle of the room with his pants down.

Sonny was grounded for assaulting the neighbor girl and stealing a handful of beef jerky sticks and a beer. After a week or so, he snuck out to meet his friends at the junk pile in the woods behind most of the houses. Sonny's friend said he wanted to B and E, which was a way they could get money and Sonny said he would do it. The other boys said they wouldn't, that it seemed dangerous, and Sonny and his friend decided to B and E a neighbor's house so they could be quick about it. They chose Paul's house. Paul was a friend, but not a good friend. They'd been over enough times to know where things were and could easily get into the house, to all the good stuff, and out, before the cops could possibly get there.

They took the back way to Paul's house and checked the garage. Empty. So they entered through the garage and snuck their way into the kitchen. They stole two beers each from the fridge. They hung them in their back pockets. Then they went into the bedroom and stole the condoms out of Paul's brother's drawer. They went into the bathroom and emptied the bottles in the cabinet into their pockets. They stuffed rags into the drains and turned on the water. They pulled a few books off the shelves. They went into the parents' bedroom and flipped through the CDs, found nothing, and started dropping the CD cases onto the ground. Sonny's friend knocked over a lamp. Sonny stepped on the lampshade. They pushed over a bookcase. Sonny took a set of earrings from a tiny box on the shelf, for Rissa.

They turned on the stove, turned on the oven. They opened the fridge and threw forks and spoons at the bottles of condiments inside. They got behind the fridge and pushed. It crashed to the ground and immediately began to leak. Brown and clear liquids seeped from the edges like from a wound. They knifed the couch pillows, turned on the fan and threw the cotton into the whirling blade. They took turns hitting the TV with an aluminum baseball bat. Sonny's friend jumped back after the blow and pretended to vibrate through and through. They could not stop laughing.

The police entered with their guns. Sonny and his friend went to a youth correctional facility in the heart of town, where they were held for six months each. Sonny wrote a letter to his parents and asked them to give it to Rissa and they did not, but they told him they did. Sonny's brother visited him one day and told him he was proud of him for doing the time and not getting into any trouble at the facility and that they were all excited for him to come home. Sonny said he was excited to come home too, because the facility was a terrible place and nobody treated him like a human being and he hated the cramped-up feelings he had all the time there, and why hadn't Mom and Dad come to visit him yet? Sonny's brother said they'd asked him to come and he'd agreed, but even he didn't like the idea of visiting Sonny out there in that place. When Sonny asked why, his brother said, "Because I hate thinking my brother deserves to be in a place like this."

Sonny didn't feel he deserved to be in a place like that. Looked at independently, the things he'd done hadn't been so bad, and he wasn't a bad person.

After six months, Sonny was released and so was his friend, but they hadn't talked much to one another in the facility, and didn't plan on doing so out of it. Sonny's parents picked him up and they went out for French fries and ice cream to celebrate because he hadn't had ice cream in forever, and the French fries in the facility tasted like a sponge.

That night he slept in his own room in his very own bed. He started high school in two months, and he was going to get a whole new wardrobe and start living a little better than he had ever imagined.

The next week, it started raining. Sonny's family lived near the center of town, where the cheaper homes were, at low elevation. After only a few days of steady rain, they received the flood warning. They were asked to leave their homes until the rains passed. They did so, and watched the houses disintegrate and wash away on the TV in the hotel room.

They had insurance. Sonny's dad had the means to keep them comfortable in the meantime. He went to work and the family started living out of room 227. Sonny and his brother slept on the floor, their parents in the full bed.

Sonny tried meth with his brother. They both liked it. They liked it a lot. They asked their parents for money, and were given it occasionally. They spent the money almost entirely on drugs. Sonny's brother had patience. He was like a Buddhist, Sonny said. Sonny started calling him Buddha. Not only because he'd put on a good deal of weight since they left their home, but also because he was remarkably in control of his cravings. When they were low on money, Sonny's brother could wait and wait, until their parents dished out a little more. Sonny would go crazy each time, not knowing when they would get more money, not knowing where, if they did, they would be able to get quality drugs. Sonny called his older brother Buddha until his older brother hit him in the mouth one afternoon while their parents were out. Sonny's brother hit him over and over again and Sonny collapsed and took the beating like a log. Sonny didn't get up. Sonny's brother rolled him over.

Sonny's brother wrapped Sonny in the hotel comforter. He stepped out of the room, looked both ways, then dragged the comforter out and down the hallway toward the stairs. He dragged it down the stairs, through the thump after thump, then to the fire exit. The door said an alarm would sound, but Sonny's brother knew it wouldn't. They'd used the exit a number of times before. The first time, Sonny had looked at the sign, then at his brother, and said, "Fuck it."

Sonny's brother dragged the comforter into the alley behind the building. He folded it, lifted it, and slid it into the dumpster. It hit the bottom like a cabbage.

Sonny's brother went back to the hotel room. There was a little blood on the carpet. He scrubbed it with one of the hotel towels and a bit of two-in-one shampoo plus conditioner. The stain lifted and he threw the towel away and phoned the front desk to request another comforter.

"For the boys," he said.

When his parents came home, Sonny's brother explained that Sonny had gone out hours before and hadn't returned.

"He had that look in his eye," Sonny's brother said.

His father nodded, though this was not an expression they'd used before in reference to anything.

Sonny's parents were up through the night waiting for him to come home, for a phone call, for anything. But nothing came.

In the morning, Sonny's father called the police. The garbage man made his rounds, stopping at each dumpster in the alley. He complained at how full they were, and Sonny's dad plugged his ears to quiet the sound of the truck and the garbage men yelling.

Sonny became a missing person. Sonny's brother got a job as the night manager at a Kmart. He got his own place. He partnered up with one of the cashiers. She had a gold tooth, but never wore jewelry. She was soft spoken. She straightened her hair with an iron. She was either slow or shy, or both, Sonny's brother couldn't tell, but she liked him. She started following him to his car.

They had a baby and got a place together on the edge of town. Sonny's brother was a hard worker; he was promoted within three months. His girlfriend hated the work, said it was exhausting. She'd already cut her hours back to take care of the baby, so he encouraged her to quit.

"The baby," he said.

They named the baby James, but Sonny's brother called the baby Rickets.

"Like Jiminy Cricket," he explained, but she still didn't like it.

When the baby was two, Sonny's brother was put in charge of a store. He had night terrors. He developed bruxism. He was very polite at work.

His girlfriend let the baby sunburn in the parking lot while she haggled over the price of a T-shirt at a street fair.

"The guy was being unreasonable," she said, and Sonny's brother tore an abstract poster from the wall. He threw a lamp, not at anyone, but at the ground by his feet. The baby was crying from the noise and from rolling onto the burns and Sonny's brother said his girlfriend was a bitch, a bitch, a bitch and that he was taking the baby and that he was leaving and good luck to her with the rest of it.

In the morning, he packed and left for work. When he got home, she'd packed the baby's things. He took the things, rented a hotel room. He stopped calling the baby Rickets and started calling the baby Sonny.

Sonny's brother rented a duplex near the Kmart he was responsible for. He applied for a loan so he could start a small business, but was declined. Sonny's brother started drinking. He thought about the drugs he used to like to do. Sonny was three.

Sonny's brother called the baby both Jiminy and Sonny. He wrote Sonny (Jiminy) on a preschool application. The teachers were excited to have a redhead. They had no other redheads. Jiminy was an adorable redhead.

Sonny's brother got letters in the mail from his ex-girlfriend asking after Rickets and Sonny's brother wrote back, *I don't call him Rickets anymore.*

Jiminy loved school. He loved playing with the other kids. When he was old enough, he started telling stories all the time to anyone who would listen. He told stories about things he'd heard other people talk about and filled in what he didn't know.

"My dad pays the electricity to a man who wants him to pay every month because that man also has to pay electricity every month but has to pay more for his electricity because he owns the machine that pumps electricity and that uses even more electricity than the machines we use in our house."

Sonny's brother wrote Jiminy's stories down and sometimes put them on the refrigerator.

"Sonny," he said, "you're a great storyteller."

Sonny's brother and Jiminy went to the park almost every day. Sonny's brother liked to watch him play and use the slide and talk to the other kids. That was something Sonny's brother had never been good at, talking to other kids, other people. He'd kept to himself most of his life, and, watching Sonny, he began to realize that he didn't like that feeling. He didn't like being surrounded by people he couldn't connect with.

"How old is yours?" he asked a woman who was sitting at the center of a bench near the swings.

"Five," she answered. She didn't move.

He sat down beside her.

"Nearly four," he said. He pointed to Jiminy at the top of the slide.

"Is your wife a redhead?"

"Girlfriend," he said, "was a redhead . . . or she *is* a redhead . . . *was* my girlfriend."

The woman made a sound like, *oh*.

"What about you?" he asked. "Your wife a redhead?"

She laughed. Her husband was.

"How long have you been married?" he asked.

"Six years—honey!"

Her daughter held a wood chip between her front teeth. She was digging for more.

"Honey, take that out of your mouth."

"He's a lucky . . ."

"Excuse me," she said.

That night, Sonny's brother watched Jiminy eat and thought about how terribly alone he was. Jiminy pressed his palm into a pile of peas.

Sonny's brother pulled out his computer and entered his information into the entry form for an online dating program. He was a single father, 6'2", 185 lb., white. He didn't like partying. He loved his son. He was interested in anything available, but wasn't desperate for a relationship. He liked music.

In the morning, he fed Jiminy. He turned on the TV and gave the boy his nebulizer. Jiminy needed fifteen minutes on the thing each morning. Jiminy watched TV and held up his nebulizer and made little noises while Sonny's brother checked his email and found three responses to his post. He wrote the same message to all three women:

You sound like a really interesting person. I'd love to meet up sometime, maybe just on the phone. Here's my number. Call whenever you like. If I'm at work, leave a message. I look forward to it.

He dropped Jiminy off at school and came home to find one voice mail from a woman named Clara. Clara wanted to talk on the phone so Sonny's brother called her and they spoke for nearly an hour. Clara also worked in retail; she was a saleswoman at Best Buy. And, yes, she had all kinds of neat home entertainment equipment as a result. Sonny's brother said he wasn't that concerned with home entertainment; his hands were full when he was at home. But he got some time away, every now and then, and he was grateful for it.

"Would you have time this weekend?" Clara asked.

He would.

Sonny's brother arranged for a sitter. He called Jiminy's school for a recommendation and they put him in touch with Kids Plus, a local service. They arranged for a sitter to arrive at four and stay until seven that night.

The sitter showed up in cutoffs and a tank top and Sonny's brother thought she couldn't have been over sixteen. She was chewing gum and as she walked through the doorway she asked if there were any songs Jiminy liked or anything like that.

"Any songs?" said Sonny's brother.

When she bent over to pick up Jiminy, Sonny's brother saw the edge of her ass dip beneath the fray of her shorts.

"I don't know," he said. "Not really. 'Puff the Magic Dragon,' " he lied.

"Really?" she asked. "That's such a sad song."

Clara was a little overweight. She'd lied on the form. It didn't matter. She liked coffee, so they went for coffee.

"You were able to get a sitter?" she asked.

"Yeah, you should have . . . she was very young. I don't know what they're thinking," he said, "sending such young women as sitters."

"I used to babysit when I was young," she said. "Women have a preternatural knack for that kind of thing. He'll be fine, I'm sure."

"How long does it take to pour two goddamn cups of coffee?" Sonny's brother said. He laughed. He bit his nails, the pointer first, then the thumb, on each hand. He spit them into his palm, lowered his hand to his side, and dropped them on the ground.

"Do you like working at Kmart?"

He didn't. But he was good at it. It was easy work. You just had to follow the rules. You had to be firm. You had to keep an eye on everything at all times. You had to be on top of everything and everyone, always.

"Yes."

The coffees arrived.

"Sorry," he said. "I'm a little nervous."

"It's cute," she said.

This, he thought, *is going well.*

After coffee, she asked him over. They sat on her couch and she put on music. She offered him wine.

"You just move through the day," he said, "tweaking your high?"

She laughed. She touched his knee. There was something charming about him, she said. He was sweet and nervous and she liked that. Most of the guys she met online were creeps. He wasn't a creep. She kissed him on the neck. It had been a long time since he'd felt a thing like that. He kissed her on the neck. She told him she knew she wanted to kiss him from the moment he'd walked into the coffee shop.

"How?" he said.

"How what?"

"How did you know?"

She leaned back and took a sip of her wine. She opened a window.

"I don't know," she said. "Maybe I didn't know. But I wanted to."

It was 6:45. He had to go. He didn't know what happened if you were late for a babysitter. He told her as much, and she said he could call. They might charge extra, but he could call. He said he would see her again, maybe later that week, and she agreed. He left her alone with the wine and the open window and he ran down to the car and called himself *stupid, stupid, stupid,* until he was finally home and walking through the door and announcing himself to the babysitter and Jiminy, who were curled up on the couch together, sleeping to a commercial for two double cheeseburgers.

Sonny's brother called Clara the next morning and she didn't answer. He called her again in the afternoon, and got nothing. He waited two days. He called her again and when she didn't answer he left a message asking how she was, how she'd been. He'd love to see her again, he said. No pressure.

Nothing.

A week later, he called for a sitter.

"The redhead," he said. "My kid's a redhead."

She arrived, sans gum, and said, " 'Puff the Magic Dragon,' right?"

Sonny's brother drove to Clara's house and saw the lights were on and so he knocked and when she came to the door she couldn't have looked more annoyed.

"What?"

"I called you," he said.

"I know," she said. "I've . . . I've been busy."

"We had a nice time," he said.

"And you left," she said.

"I have a kid."

"You could have called and had the sitter stay a little longer," she said. "I used to be a babysitter and I know you could have, but you didn't want to."

"So you've been ignoring my calls?"

"Yes."

He left.

When he arrived home, he found the sitter and Jiminy sitting on the floor in the living room, an entire box of Legos splayed between the sitter's two widespread legs. Jiminy was at her feet, pressing the blocks together.

"Will you have sex with me for money?" Sonny's brother said.

The babysitter looked up. Jiminy looked up.

"For how much?" she asked.

Sonny's brother used Kids Plus once a week. Then twice a week. At first, "The redhead." Then, "Jen."

"I don't do this with anybody else," she explained. It didn't matter.

Not really. That's what he liked about it. Her time was her time. For a few hours a week, she was on *their* time. As long as she wasn't doing it with other men while she was on *their* time, it didn't matter.

"It doesn't matter," he said.

"One time, Dad was at work and someone told him she was going to call his supervisor because Dad is an overemotional worker and then Dad was worried for a long time because what if she did that, and he thought he was going to get fired and then he didn't get fired."

"Is that true," she asked. "Are you an overemotional worker?"

"Sometimes," he said. "I guess I am."

"Like when?"

"Dad turned off the gas one time because fuck the gas company and . . ."

"Jiminy," Sonny's brother said, "language."

"And—sorry—and they didn't turn off the gas so we got free gas for a month and then he started paying again."

"That's nice of you," she said. "Can I smoke in here?"

"No," Sonny's brother said.

"Then I've got to go."

"You should stay," said Sonny's brother.

"Can't smoke in here," she said.

❀

Sonny's brother liked to come on the babysitter's belly. He liked to see it run the length of her. He liked her to lie back, to let him decorate her.

"What are you doing tomorrow?" she asked from the shower. He made her leave the door open when she used the bathroom, for whatever reason. He didn't know her that well. He left it at that.

"Why?" he asked. He was prone, in bed.

"Don't get all freaked out," she said. "Kids Plus is having a customer picnic. Looking to recruit some new folks and feed some regulars."

"You want me there to boast the lengths you'll go to keep the kids happy?"

"I just meant to say there'd be free food there, and free drinks, and lots of kids for Jiminy to meet and you don't have to be a shithead."

The shower shut off and she entered the bedroom in a yellow towel. He tugged at the towel's edge.

"What have you got under there?"

"He's a good kid, and he likes people," she said.

"I don't know where he gets it from."

He began to kiss her neck.

"Have you thought about starting a family?"

He pulled the towel away.

"A wife? Another kid?"

"Yeah," he said, "that's good. Keep it up. Ask me about life insurance."

He pulled her down to the bed, laid her on her back. He kissed her stomach, her neck, her ears. He ran his hands along the side of her head and moved down, kissing as he went.

"Jiminy could use a sibling, maybe. A sister," she said. He lightly thumbed her throat. "Or a brother."

He kissed her between her legs. She whispered something. He pinched her nipple. He took his time, though the clock was running. She came and he pulled back, he hit her once across the face. Then again. He hit her again, in the chest. She started screaming.

She screamed, "What the fuck?" and he hit her again. He hit her again and again and again and she reached beside her and grabbed the lamp and threw it at him, as hard as she could. It didn't break, but it hit his arm and chest hard and fell onto the bed. She sat up and lifted the lamp with both hands and hit him in the face, on the back of the head, and again. He fell into the bed, face first and she hit him again and again and again until he rose up and batted the lamp away. She leapt from the bed, darted to the door.

"You motherfucker," she said.

Jiminy said, "Dad?" from the other room.

"You piece of shit," she said.

He was breathing hard, bleeding and breathing and hunched over on the bed. She backed up toward the door then paused. She picked up an aluminum baseball bat from where it was propped against the bookcase. She swung once, landed the blow on the side of his head.

"You piece of shit."

She swung again. She swung until her arms went limp and Jiminy was pushing the door open. She pushed the door back.

"Just a second, sweetie," she said.

"Dad?"

"He's sleeping," she said. "Just a second."

Jiminy was less social in grade school. He didn't seem interested in girls. He did well on the tests, on his homework. He didn't like to talk in the halls. During recess, he swung his arms. He moved around underneath the monkey bars and swung his arms and made smashing sounds. He went to a small school. The other kids were nice enough. Most of them, anyway. But he avoided them. He was quiet in class too, didn't take well to being called on, asked for an answer. Every now and then, he cried. The teachers brought his foster parents in, told them their son was having trouble *fitting in.* He was exhibiting an unhealthy level of reticence. Jiminy's foster parents were grateful for the notice. They'd asked to be alerted as to his social adjustments. They were worried for him, not about him.

"Jim," they said. "We'd like to invite some of your friends over this weekend."

He didn't want them to.

"We think it would be nice to have a few friends over, Jim."

"No," he said.

"Just a few," said his foster mother.

She made the calls. Jiminy cried in his bedroom. His foster father stood outside the door.

"Son," he said. "Your mother and I think it will be good for you to see your friends outside of school. You'll be able to have more fun."

"I don't have any friends," Jiminy said.

"Some of your classmates, then," said his foster father, "who will become your friends."

"The Millers can't," said Jiminy's foster mother. "But the Jones boy is coming and . . . Susie Parker."

"Hear that?"

Nothing.

That weekend Susie Parker and Sam Jones came over to Jiminy's new house. The three of them sat in the patio furniture and ate chips and Sam asked,

"What's that?" He pointed to Jiminy's treehouse.

Jiminy shrugged.

"It's a treehouse," Susie said. "Can we climb it?"

Jiminy shrugged again. He crumbled a chip in his hand, scattered the flakes onto the table.

"Mr. Legit, can we climb the tree house?" Sam said.

"Of course," said Jiminy's foster father.

"I'll have to show you how," Jiminy said.

Underneath the tree house, Jiminy loosed a rope from between two low branches of a nearby tree. He threw the rope up, knocked down the stepladder, which came down swinging. They each took a step back, and Jiminy reached out, grabbed the ladder and began to climb.

Susie and Sam followed.

The treehouse was dark inside, shaded. There were milk crates to sit on, books to read. There was a board game, Monopoly, missing all of the money and most of the pieces.

"What do you do up here?" asked Susie.

"I think about you," Jiminy said.

Susie blushed. She touched a bow on her sock. Sam Jones laughed.

"That's not all he does," he said.

Jiminy looked at Sam and said, "You can leave."

"I don't want to leave," said Sam Jones.

"Then you have to be nicer."

That evening, Jiminy's foster mother lit some citronella candles and they all gathered around the picnic table and ate brisket and macaroni and mashed potatoes and coleslaw and watched the fireflies stir as the sun went down.

"Can we go to the haunted van?" Jiminy asked.

His foster mother paused. She looked at her son, looked him in the eyes, and Jiminy shifted in his seat.

"Next time, Sonny."

"The haunted van?" Susie asked.

"Next time," Jiminy said.

"When is next time?" asked Sam Jones.

"We'll have to talk with your parents, but next weekend?" Jiminy's foster mother said. "Sunday is family day and homework day. And Jiminy does his studies during the week."

"How about next Saturday?" said Jiminy.

His foster parents stood by the grill together.

"That's just fine," said his foster father.

The next weekend, Sam Jones and Susie Parker came over to investigate the haunted van. Jiminy led them out the back door and into a field. They pulled apart the wire of a barbed-wire fence and climbed through to the other side. They wandered, as the grass grew taller. They walked for nearly half an hour before Susie asked,

"How much further?"

"Not much," said Jiminy, "It's just right around here somewhere."

They reached a creek. They went down to the creek's edge. It was narrow enough to cross, but they were going to get wet.

"You have to cross," said Jiminy.

Sam started walking. He stepped into the water and kept on until he was calf deep.

"I don't want to," Susie said.

Sam and Jiminy shrugged.

"Stay right there, then," Jiminy said.

Sam and Jiminy crossed the creek. They walked up the creek bed and climbed over the edge. There were woods ahead of them, and taller grass. They walked on. They walked for nearly fifteen minutes before Jiminy said,

"There is no haunted van."

"Okay," said Sam. "Then what are we even doing out here?"

"I don't know," said Jiminy. "Are you mad?"

"No," said Sam. "Liar."

"Can we scare Susie and tell her we saw ghosts?" asked Jiminy.

Sam said, "Yes."

The two of them ran back toward the creek, they bolted across the water, caught Susie off guard, and told her to run, run for her life, run as fast as she could. The three of them darted back across the field. Sam and Jiminy screamed at the top of their lungs. Susie began to scream too. She began to cry. She kept running. They climbed through the barbed-wire fence. Susie was breathing heavily, she was screaming and crying and the boys were screaming and holding back laughter and they all ran into Jiminy's foster parents' house and collapsed into the living room. They screamed from their collapsed positions and Sam and Jiminy rolled around while Susie lay on her stomach screaming into the carpet. Jiminy's foster father appeared in the living room asking,

"What's wrong? What's wrong? What's happened?" over and over again until Jiminy stopped screaming and said nothing was wrong, they were just playing.

"What's wrong with her?" asked Jiminy's foster father.

Susie was crying and curled up and covering her head.

"What happened, Sonny?"

"Nothing happened, Dad, we just scared her a little."

"We were just playing, Mr. Legit, honest."

"Susie," said Jiminy's foster father. "Susie, hon, what's wrong?"

She wouldn't uncurl.

"We were just playing," said Sam.

Sam and Jiminy went into middle school together and then high school. They started drinking together and traded porn until Sam had sex, then kept having sex, and Jiminy was left to his own devices. When they were seniors, they got tattoos. They did well in high school. They did what they wanted, for the most part. Sam was popular and Jiminy was Sam's friend. Sam played baseball and had late night baseball parties. Jiminy hit on his baseball friends. Jiminy let the varsity pitcher fuck him on the washing machine at Sam's house. The pitcher's girlfriend found out about it and painted FAGGOT on Jiminy's car in pink spray paint. Jiminy outlined it in gold.

"You're gay?" asked his foster father.

"I think so," he said.

"Your mother's not going to like it."

"She'll get over it."

Jiminy got the pitcher's number from Sam. Sam was reluctant, told Jiminy to let it go, but Jiminy insisted. He called the pitcher at all hours of the night until finally the pitcher told him to meet him where Collins Road met Fair, just outside of town. Jiminy brought an aluminum baseball bat.

The pitcher was there, sitting on the roof of his car when Jiminy arrived.

"You've got to stop calling me," said the pitcher.

"Start answering," said Jiminy.

"I'm already in enough trouble as it is," said the pitcher. "Just leave me alone, okay?"

"You want me to leave you alone?"

"I'm asking you to leave me alone," said the pitcher.

Jiminy thought about the baseball bat. He thought about the washer, the spray paint, Sam.

"Fine," he said.

Jiminy bought opium for the first time from an Irish guy at a Mexican bar.

"How do I know it's real?" he asked.

"Smell it," said the Irish guy, "smoke it. It's real." He pocketed the money.

Jiminy smoked opium on the roof of a used bookstore in the middle of downtown. He felt sleepy, but not tired. Things seemed a little easier. He thought he saw the pitcher's truck. It didn't matter. He was on the roof. He thought he saw a shooting star. He wasn't sure. There was an ant on the back of his hand.

In the morning, he would take better notes. He would become a straight-A student, because, what the fuck, why not? Everything else was shitty, why not kick ass in school and let everyone go fuck themselves?

He took better notes. He did a little better. Not a lot, but a little. He smoked opium on the roofs of old buildings, anything with a fire escape. Sam came a few times, said he didn't like it. It didn't do anything, really. Just slowed him down. Sam was into activity all of a sudden. Jiminy preferred to relax. He aced a few tests. His parents were proud. He was in love with opium.

When the Irish guy disappeared, Jiminy bought oxycodone from a friend of Sam's. That knocked him on his ass. He couldn't take much of it at all. Sometimes he threw up. Other times, he passed out, or fell.

Jiminy's foster father had a heart attack. They visited him in the hospital and Jiminy pocketed some of his heart medication. He took it with a beer. He took great notes. Aced another test. He took the heart medication with a glass of absinthe.

"It's real," Sam swore. "It's imported."

They both took the heart medication. They got drunk on absinthe, forewent the ritual and drank it straight from the bottle.

Jiminy kissed Sam and Sam kissed him back for a second. Then he stopped.

Jiminy took more of the heart medication and Sam drank more of the absinthe.

Sam copied Jiminy's answers on an English test and they both aced the test together.

They graduated from high school and went to a number of parties afterward. They were both drunk and driving from one end of town to the other. They filled the car with girls Sam was interested in. Jiminy was rude to all of them. He started crying halfway through the night and locked himself in the bathroom at one of the parties. He took all of the oxycodone he had and passed out. He woke up in the emergency room, passed out again. He woke up strapped to a bed. He passed out again.

He was in a facility. He'd tried to kill himself. He hadn't actually, but that's what they told him.

His foster mother came to visit. She looked like a ghost. She didn't look real. She told him his room was exactly how he'd left it. There was food waiting for him when he got home. She was happy to see him with a little color in his cheeks. She started crying. She always cried. He told her he didn't mean to kill himself and that made her cry even harder.

Sam came to visit and said Jiminy needed to curb his drinking.

"I'm worried about you."

Sam went to college out of state. He played baseball until he hurt his shoulder. Then he coached. He had three daughters.

Jiminy and Sam talked on the phone once a month or so. Jiminy got a job cleaning pools. He could smoke while he worked, show up drunk from the night before, if necessary. Jiminy liked an easy job. Sam wanted a hard job, and it broke him. Neither of them were what they had expected, but they didn't know what they had expected.

Jiminy got a girlfriend with a dead tooth. She laughed all the time, at almost everything he said. And he liked that most of the time. He liked saying something and her laughing and feeling good about himself even when he didn't know the best thing to say. She also liked to party. So they drank a lot and screwed a lot and things were good in that way. She screwed around too but it didn't matter because Jiminy always imagined that he would screw around too, as soon as he met the right guy. It was easier being with a girl who laughed all the time. She let him do what he wanted to her anyway, so things were good enough for the time being.

"Sounds like a winner," Sam said.

"Fuck you," said Jiminy. "Are we even friends anymore?"

Jiminy broke into the morgue and stole a jar of formaldehyde and started dipping his cigarettes in it. He had dreams that he was swimming in a pool of come and woke up on the job in the customer's pool, as they were pulling in from wherever they'd been. He climbed out, he'd slipped. He was awful sorry about it. The customer shook his head and carried the brown paper bag full of groceries into the house. He called to cancel the regular service and when Jiminy was asked why, he said he couldn't understand it.

"He said you were swimming in his pool," said Raul, owner of Deep Blue.

"Well, I wasn't," said Jiminy.

Jiminy was put on probation at work and he resented it and started staying up later than usual and trying to say mean things to his girlfriend so she wouldn't laugh, but she laughed anyway, most of the time, until she finally said, "You don't want me around, do you?" and he knew exactly what he could say back, the one thing she couldn't possibly laugh at, and he said, "No, I don't," and she started laughing and laughing while she packed and spilled her drink and laughed some more and left.

A couple of weeks later she came back to their old apartment and knocked and no one answered, so she used her old keys to let herself in, and she discovered Jiminy slumped in the center of the room, nearly two weeks dead. The phone was ringing. She picked it up to dial 911 and Raul was on the other end. There was a problem with Jiminy's last paycheck. He hadn't signed the time sheet and they couldn't pay him until he did.

"Jiminy's dead," said his ex-girlfriend, "I think. But I need the paycheck. I'm pregnant."

Raul said she would have to come in.

"What happened to you?" asked Raul. "You used to be so lighthearted, and you're so serious. So sad."

"I'm pregnant," she said. "And I come home to find the father dead in the living room."

"It's sad, yes," said Raul. "But maybe Jiminy would not have been the best role model? Maybe he could have pulled things together, yes. But who knows? You are a very beautiful woman. You will find another man to love you and take care of you and you need not be so sad. Life is very good."

"I'm broke," she said.

"You'll come work for me," he said.

"Really?"

"You'll be a secretary and coordinator. You'll organize the schedules, assign my boys jobs they can work in succession. One after the other, huh? Less driving around, wasting time. You've done this kind of thing before?"

"Of course," she lied. She laughed when they shook hands. He smiled.

Raul brought her gifts throughout the day. Chocolates, jewelry found in public pools. He told her she was doing a great job. She started to show after three months. After six, people began to say she was *full-blown pregnant.*

She was great at her job. She had a knack for working Raul's boys to the bone. For the most part they liked taking orders from her. They liked how clean her plans were. She organized things by neighborhood and by the type of job request. Cleaners went out in a caravan, and the de-cloggers went on specialty missions, house by house. There was no overlap, and no crew had to switch gear. She was an expert.

Raul admired her hair, her dress. He gave her a raise and said it was for work wear. He thought she deserved to look more professional. She bought a pair of shoes. While she leaned over to drink at the water fountain, he placed his hand on the small of her back. She rose into it. Neither of them said anything.

At eight months, she went on leave. Raul came to visit her at home. He brought her items she needed from the store when she wasn't up to it. He rubbed her feet while she pried open a jar of mayonnaise.

They watched television together when he was tired from a day at work without her and she was lonely from day after day of being by herself in Jiminy's old apartment. Raul was there when the baby was born.

He drove her home. He was enthralled, had never seen anything like it.

"You were so strong," he said.

She was busy with the baby, just watching it. That thing had come out of her. That little thing, moving around and looking at nothing in particular. It seemed strange to hold it. She'd held it so well the months before, and now it was in her hands and making her nervous. Raul paced in front of them. He wanted to see more. He wanted to be a doctor, be a nurse on the maternity ward, be a gynecologist, be a dad. He got down on one knee.

"Will you marry me?" he asked.

She lifted her arms, settled the baby's head against her upper arm. The thing kept shifting, readjusting, so she had to shift and readjust as well. She couldn't get entirely comfortable. She was nervous about the thing's fragility. The baby coughed and foam came out.

"Yes," she said. She wiped the foam away with her sleeve.

They moved in together. She stayed on maternity leave and worked a little from home. Raul brought her the schedules and she coordinated things in her off hours, which were few. He watched the baby and sent her to the dentist. He fixed her dead tooth. She didn't laugh like she used to, but things were better then they'd ever been. She was safe. She had a home. She had a family. She missed the casual fun of a guy like Jiminy. She missed the danger, too. She missed fighting. She and Raul never fought. Even when she pushed him—nothing.

They had more children: two girls and another boy. The children all had dark skin, like their father. Jiminy's son, Osiris, was a pale red-head. The two girls grew up the best of friends. Osiris and his brother, Michael, did not get along. They fought over toys. They fought over food. They fought over space on the carpet.

"That is what boys do," said Raul.

"It's not all they do," insisted Jiminy's ex-girlfriend.

Michael was two years younger than Osiris, but twice his size. At three, Michael sat on Osiris's arm in the backyard and broke two of his fingers. Michael did not want to tell his parents and Osiris cried and cried while Michael pretended to play in the grass. Eventually Raul came home from work and found Osiris crying, his hand swollen like a ripe fruit, and he rushed him to the hospital. Raul spanked Michael. Raul was a big fan of spanking. He spanked Michael until Michael was through crying. Raul asked Michael, over and over again, between spankings, if he knew why this was happening, and Michael said, yes, because he'd hurt Osiris, and Raul said, "Yes, you hurt him very badly."

Michael and Osiris grew up at odds. Michael went to a private school, Osiris to a specialty school. He was slower than the other kids. He had trouble holding on to an idea, trouble forming sentences, trouble speaking in public. He was diagnosed with mild autism, dyslexia. He wore glasses and had a stutter. Raul was a very kind father to him. He patted the boy on the head when they were at the table. He held him in his lap while they watched movies or TV.

Michael told his mother he felt lonely. He did not think his dad loved him as much as Osiris.

"Your father loves you both," she said, "equally."

She was in bed when she said it. She spent most of the day in bed. She took pills from a series of jars at the bedside. She had trouble standing up, trouble walking. There was something off in her hips. Raul waited on her hand and foot. He also worked overtime with the kids. He brought them to school, picked them up. He made dinner for the family, and made sure to spend some time with them between homework and bedtime. She admired Raul. She admired his determination, his strength. She did not want to go back to work. The idea of more scheduling and rescheduling was appalling.

"You don't have to work," said Raul. "But you do need to help with the house, with the children. You cannot sleep late all the time, and shut yourself away. It's not fair to me or to them."

"Your father picks favorites," she later told Michael. "You must have done something to upset him."

Michael remembered the spanking, Osiris's hand. He was extra nice to his sisters. He played with them even when he didn't want to.

One afternoon, Michael helped them dig a hole in the backyard and fill it with water from the hose attached to the back of the house. They dug the hole a few feet deep with a shovel they'd found in the garage.

"Goddamnit," said Raul when he got home from work. "Look what you've done."

He found his wife in the bed, asleep.

"Have you seen what your children did to the lawn?" he asked.

She stirred, rolled, drew a pillow between her knees.

"No."

"They are destroying the lawn," he said. "They have destroyed the lawn."

"And you worked so hard on that lawn," she said.

"Don't talk shit to me. I worked very hard on the lawn. I want us to have a respectable house, to be a respectable family. I do not want us to live in filth and have filthy things. We do not need that, and I won't have it." He went outside and yelled for the children to get out of the hole, to rinse off. He would bring them towels. This was not right, he explained. They were doing harm.

They were laughing and covered in mud and beautiful to look at, he realized. They were grounded, he told them. One week each. Everyone except for Osiris, who had been in the house for most of it, though he had helped start the hole earlier that afternoon.

That night, Michael punched Osiris in the nose while he was sleeping. Osiris started bleeding and yelling and crying and Raul burst into the bedroom and grabbed Michael by both shoulders, lifted him, carried him into the living room where he yanked down the boy's shorts and spanked him and spanked him and spanked him. Michael was a sobbing, snotty mess in the center of the room when Raul left. He dabbed peroxide on Osiris's nose. He stuffed the bleeding hole with tissue. He came back out into the living room to find Michael sitting upright, leaned against the wall.

"I hate you," Michael said. "I want to kill you."

Raul went into the kitchen. He poured himself a drink and sat at the table. The boy did not want to kill him, he told himself. He poured himself another drink. The boy could not kill him if he tried.

Raul climbed into bed beside his wife.

"What is wrong?" he asked.

That made her curl tighter.

"How are you?" he tried.

"I'm fine," she said, and curled.

"What can I do for you?" he said. "You seem unhappy."

"I am unhappy," she said.

"What can I do for you?"

" . . . "

"What can I do for you, my love?"

"Not everything is about you."

She was alone in her room most of the time. She cut her fingernails short. Too short. She pulled on the ends of her hair until strands came loose between her fingers. She thought, *Maybe I should go to a doctor*, and took handful after handful of Tylenol, Advil, ibuprofen. What was wrong with her? She didn't like to think about it. Maybe Jiminy had gotten her sick. Maybe he was a deeply disturbed person and that had infected her somehow. During the day, when her kids were at school and her husband was at work, she felt almost at peace. But the moment they all arrived home, the house was in an uproar and the noise did not stop until late in the night when it was replaced by the sound of Raul flipping through channel after channel until he fell asleep. This was not what she expected.

She sued Raul for custody of their four kids, and she won. She told her lawyer that Raul struck the children, he played favorites, he did not get enough sleep, and he was often cruel to her and the others. Michael testified that Raul had indeed struck him. Osiris was very overwhelmed by the witness stand, the court proceedings. He wept openly before the judge, his parents, the court. The two daughters both said that they loved their parents. Their mom and their dad. They loved them.

She kept Jiminy's apartment. Raul wasn't allowed within one hundred feet.

Outside of the courtroom he called her a snake and a bitch and said she would not get away with it. He said she would murder their children. He said this was a death sentence.

But the truth was, she was much happier without him around. She woke up with the kids, took them to school. She received checks from Raul, checks from the government, and she was able to feed the children and herself, to keep them clothed. At home, she cleaned from time to time. She learned how to darn socks, how to fix a hem.

Raul sent letters with the checks, asked how the kids were, how Osiris was adjusting to middle school. She didn't write back. He was allowed to visit once a month. He would find out then.

Raul went back to cleaning pools. He spent less and less time managing the place, and more and more time out on jobs. He went alone. He spent hours on a single job. His boys started taking their time too. Raul was gone all the time, so they felt less pressure to perform. Deep

Blue lost business. Raul cleaned and smoked cigarettes. He skimmed the pools over and over again with a bluish net at the end of a long handle. He walked slowly along the edge of the pool then back again, delicately.

Raul pounded on Jiminy's old apartment door. It was nearly midnight. The TV was on at high volume. Raul pounded and yelled and wanted his kids back and his life back and his ex-wife didn't answer, but turned up the TV instead. He saw Michael in the window and he waved to him. Michael disappeared.

Raul went home. Raul enlisted in the army. He went to training camp only two months later. He slept better than he had in years. He woke up early. He worked out. He learned about a variety of weapons. He ate the minimum amount. Lost weight, gained very little muscle. Deep Blue was in the hands of his top guy, Joe. Joe did fine, kept the company afloat. Raul went to war.

Raul was the gunner in the second Humvee in a caravan. One morning, they came across what appeared to be an abandoned village. Their translator announced their presence. He warned the occupants to come out, unarmed. No one responded. They fired warning shots into the dirt by one of the larger buildings on the town's perimeter. Nothing. The caravan entered the village.

Osiris's mom made him an apple pie from scratch for his birthday. She worked in the kitchen all the time now. She was always trying things out. She brought friends over two or three nights a week. They tried drink recipes from magazines. They tried different fruits and vegetables in different shapes, pressed against different parts of their bodies. Cucumber slivers over their eyes, carrot skins down the length of their arms and legs. They rubbed avocado into their palms and over their hands. They drank pink drinks and purple drinks and brown drinks with clear drinks dropped into them. Several of her friends came to Osiris's birthday party. They had a special punch in a bowl on the counter. Osiris ate three slices of pie. Michael had one. His sisters had none. One sister had fattened up, while the other had grown very skinny. His fat sister was moody, but laughed a lot like his mother. His skinny sister was very shy at home, but extremely popular in school. The skinny sister did not like to be around food. The fat sister did not like to be around people and food. She took a slice of pizza to her bedroom. The skinny sister asked to have some of the punch and her mother poured her a very small glass.

"It's sweet," said the skinny sister.

Her mother winked.

Osiris sat back in his chair. He unbuttoned his pants, as he'd seen men do in movies. He reached his hand into his pants, as was suddenly his inclination. One of his mother's friends saw and looked away. She made a little sound like a rush of air. She drank some of her punch. Osiris burped and his mother turned and she said,

"Osiris!"

She immediately regretted this, though, as it caused everyone in the room to turn and discover Osiris, his hand buried deep beneath the waistline of his striped boxers, where he shuffled and tugged at himself, watching them drink their punch.

His mother grabbed him by the arm and pulled him out of the chair and into the other room.

"Not here," she said. Her eyes were a little slow in following the direction of her face. "Go to your room if you're done being in public. Don't embarrass me."

Osiris went into his room and his fat sister was there, eating her pizza.

"Michael is using my TV," she said.

Osiris said he wanted private time and his fat sister explained again that Michael was in her room, watching TV, and she needed a place to be.

Osiris walked over to her and plucked the pizza from her hand. He dropped it onto the carpet, pressed his foot into the cheese and toppings. He twisted his foot into the pizza and said, "Get out."

His fat sister started to cry.

"I'm hungry," she said.

"You're fat," said Osiris.

The military men rang the doorbell. Osiris's mother answered the door and listened and took the paperwork and the flag and went back into the kitchen and told her friends her husband was dead.

"You're married?" said a friend. She scooped a citrus wedge with the punch spoon and dropped it into her cup.

Michael asked what happened. The skinny sister asked what happened to Dad? The fat sister wandered in, checked the box for more pizza.

Their mother said they were broke. Osiris's skinny sister, Magdalene,
got a job at Sonic. She wore roller skates, got tipped extra. She hated
working there, thought she would get fat by just breathing the air.
She considered working there for five hours the equivalent of two full
meals. She walked to and from work. She walked the neighborhood.
She flirted with the boys at Sonic. She gave a few of them handjobs
after work. But she didn't really like the boys at Sonic, so she stopped.
When the summer came, college boys started showing up at Sonic.
She worked later shifts, talked to the college boys. She liked older
men because they had more to say than younger men. They made
jokes, but didn't just make jokes. They said things like, "I'd really like
to show you it," about the town where they grew up, or places they'd
seen when they traveled. They said things like, "You'll see one day,"
and, "When you go there, make sure you . . ." These moments were
the highlights of her shift.

She liked television. She watched several hours of television a day. She
preferred stories in which the female lead exhibited confidence and
charm. Her mother always talked about charisma, how Michael had
charisma. Magdalene liked when the female lead acted like her brother Michael. They were all in high school together. Osiris did not do
well socially or academically. He remained in special classes. Michael
got by on his charm, for the most part. He played team sports. That
meant a lot. He kept his grades up, somehow. They weren't great, but
they were good enough. He ran track. He was voted *Nicest* his senior
year. Magdalene had a certain following too. Claire, the fat sister, was
miserable in school and at home. She spent hours with Osiris, though
he was almost always mean to her and moody.

Magdalene went home with one of the college boys. He gave her a drug in a white pill and he took one too. The next morning she was achy all over and thirsty and a little sad, but she got dressed and snuck out without waking him. His name was either Tim or Jim and he was a hunky linguistics major. She felt a little like a strong female lead, leaving as she did. She walked home and felt better by the time she was halfway there. She stopped at the Sonic on the way, checked her schedule. She had the day off, the next day too. It was rare they gave her weekends off, so she planned to make the best of it.

When she got home, her mother was waiting for her. Osiris and Claire were in the courtyard between the apartments, arguing. Michael had been out all night as well.

"Are you using protection?" asked their mother.

"Mom," said Magdalene.

"Sit down."

Magdalene sat. She crossed her legs, looked at her hands.

"Are you?"

Magdalene shook her head.

"Jesus, Maggie. Look. Do you know your options? Do you even know what you're doing? How much do you know?"

Magdalene shrugged. She pinched her belly.

"I need to take a shower," she said.

"Look, Honey," her mother placed her hands on her daughter's. "You just need to think it through is all."

Magdalene nodded.

"Do you know how to use a condom?"

She shrugged. "Don't they need to know that?"

"You need to know it too," said her mother. "Do you want to go on the pill? Do you know what that is?"

"I know what it does, Mom."

"It does more than you think it does."

"I know what it does," she said.

"Jesus Christ, Maggie. Oh Lord-God-Jesus-Christ and fucking piss."

That weekend Magdalene hid white wine in a water bottle and drank it in the grass by the public pool. She undid her top and lay on her belly. A young boy approached her and asked if she would turn over and she said, "Scram, you little pervert," even though part of her thought it might have been a fun thing to do.

Osiris and Claire had come to the pool with her, and they swam while she continued to sunbathe and drink more white wine. From a distance the boy yelled, "You're dumb as rocks."

She put her head down, closed her eyes.

Osiris peed in the pool and told Claire and she got out and spent the afternoon in the shade of the public pool's one tree, crying and prodding the ant piles with sticks she pulled loose from the branches. Osiris got out too and sat by Magdalene. He explained that he liked the water because it had shape and it didn't have shape and he could move all around inside of it, but it still held him up. He could close his eyes and sink himself and feel it all around him. He felt in and out of control.

Magdalene drank the entire bottle of white wine while Osiris talked to her.

"I peed in the pool," he said.

She took sip after sip.

After the wine was gone, Magdalene said they had to go. Osiris followed her willingly, but Claire refused to get up.

"Fine," said Magdalene. "Osiris . . . "

They left together. Claire stayed under the tree poking the ants, convinced they would come back. Magdalene left with no intention of coming back. She and her half brother left the neighborhood in which the pool was located and wandered downtown. They stopped in a thrift store and went through the old records. Osiris found an old candy cane in a chest beneath a pile of sweaters and he put it in his pocket and broke off piece after piece, which he ate when he was convinced no one was looking. Magdalene found a dress she liked. It was white, with a floral pattern around the collar. She held it up against her in front of the mirror. Osiris said it looked nice. There was something in his mouth.

"What are you eating?"

Osiris shrugged. He went over to a box of toys and thumbed the G.I. Joes. Magdalene shoved the dress into her purse and grabbed Osiris by the elbow. She pulled him toward the door and he started to cry because he wanted to take the G.I. Joes with him but Magdalene explained that you do not always get the things you want in life, though she did not use those words exactly.

"Is he okay?" asked the clerk as she dragged him past the counter.

"He's fine," she said. "He's retarded."

Outside, Osiris bit her on the wrist.

"I'm not retarded," he said.

"You're dumb as rocks," Magdalene said. She rubbed her wrist, cursed him a few more times, and started to walk in the opposite direction. She wasn't headed anywhere in particular, just away from him.

Osiris picked up a rock by his foot and threw it at his older sister. She was already off balance, teetering from the adrenaline of the recent theft plus the bottle of wine on an empty stomach. When the rock struck, she collapsed. She hit the sidewalk like an egg. Her sweaty body made a soft smack, and she lay there, still, until Osiris finally approached. He was afraid, afraid of what she might do and of what he might have done. He wasn't a violent boy, wasn't typically angry about much, but he'd lost control. She rolled over and looked up at her brother. She started crying and told him she was pregnant and he started crying because he didn't want to hurt the baby.

"You can't tell Mom," she said, and he swore he wouldn't.

That night she drank another bottle of white wine. She hated the taste of white wine but thought it would undo the pregnancy, so she drank it down like medicine. The police brought Claire home. She'd refused to leave the pool after closing and no one knew exactly where she came from or where she was going and she'd been too scared to tell them at first, but eventually one of the cops brought her a Red Rocket ice cream and she told them where she was from and where she was going and why she had refused to leave.

"You her sister?" the officer asked Magdalene. Their mother was asleep in the back room and the doorbell hadn't waked her. At least that's what Magdalene hoped.

"I'm her sister, yes. Our mother's asleep, but you can be sure we're all happy to see Claire alive and well and . . . "

"We'd prefer to talk with a legal guardian," explained the officer. "It would put our minds at ease to know her mother's assured of her safety."

"Well, she's sleeping," explained Magdalene.

Michael's car pulled up behind the police car, its lights still awhirl, and Michael climbed out and hurried to the front door.

"What happened?"

"You're the brother?"

"Claire refused to leave the pool and they called the cops on her," explained Magdalene. "Now they want to talk to Mom."

"Wake her up," said Michael. Michael talked to the police while Magdalene went to get their mother.

"Mom," Magdalene said. She put a hand on either of her mother's shoulders. "Mom. Get up."

Their mother didn't budge.

"Mom, the cops are here. Everything's fine. They just brought Claire home because she wouldn't leave the pool."

Nothing.

"Mom." Magdalene shook their mother until her head began to bounce against the pillow. She looked around her for an empty bottle, liquor or pills. There was nothing. She shook her mother again.

"Stop it," said their mother.

Magdalene's hands came off.

"Your brother's taking care of it."

Magdalene realized then that the lights from the police car had shut off. The front door closed. Michael was talking to either Claire or Osiris. He made a joke. Claire erupted with hearty laughter.

"Do you have something you want to tell me?"

"No . . . Claire wouldn't leave, so we left . . ."

"You're pregnant. Osiris told me."

"So? So what?"

"That's why you've been stealing all the white wine? All the bourbon?"

She hadn't been stealing bourbon.

"It won't work," said her mother. "You're going to shit out a baby that's more retarded than you or whoever you let do this to you." Her mother sat up. "Sit down," she said.

Magdalene sat. She put her hands on her lap.

"Stop drinking. Start taking care of yourself. Do you know this boy at all?"

Magdalene shook her head.

"Okay. Does Michael know yet?"

She shook her head again.

"Okay."

When Magdalene had the baby, she had to quit Sonic. Michael got a job at a hardware store. He worked the morning hours. Their mother started selling their belongings online. Almost every appliance in the house was for sale. They had to be extra careful. If it wasn't screwed down or attached to a pipe or vent, she photographed it and put it online. Their sheets, their pillows, their toys, their microwave. All of it. The only exception was the television. They were tired all the time—they needed to relax. Plus, when the baby came, there was going to be a lot of stillness, a lot of time confined to a single room, and they would need something to get them through it. They sold the video games on the first day. The microwave, in a week. They sold all of Claire's stuffed animals and she was sad to see them go, but was excited for the baby.

"For the baby," said their mother.

"For the baby," said Claire. She handed over her stuffed fox.

"For the baby," said their mother.

"For the baby," said Michael. He folded his leather jacket, placed it in the box.

"For the baby," said their mother.

"For William," said Magdalene. She took out her earrings. She borrowed her mother's old tops. She learned to make microwave popcorn on the stove. She cut her hair. She cancelled her plans for the tattoo at her ankle. She got her rest. She did not drink. She did everything her mother told her to do, everything she imagined her father might. She remembered her father. She saw him as a hero. A veteran. He'd fought so William could have the kind of life they'd always dreamed of having. Her father had died for that opportunity. She would die for it too. More than that, she would live.

William was born at seven pounds three ounces. As his mother remembered it, he was born fist raised to the air as if in mid-charge. It was a painful birth, she had forty-two stitches, but she hardly remembered them. She held William for nearly an hour after they cleaned him up without saying a word. He had blue eyes, a shroud of brown hair. He cried a little, but she could tell it was only because he hadn't learned the right words for the situation.

They brought the baby home and Claire loved the baby and Osiris loved the baby and their mother loved the baby and Michael was willing to help out here and there. When the baby was sleeping, everyone in the house was quiet. If Claire and Osiris got into it, it only took a gesture from their mother to send them outside where they could fight as loud as they wanted without disturbing the baby. The baby worked a kind of magic on the house. He charmed nearly everyone who entered. The baby's grandmother started laughing like she did when she was much younger. There was a smile on her face nearly all of the time. His grandmother laughed and laughed, at nearly everything he did. His mother was weepy a lot of the time. She'd wanted him gone. She'd nearly lost him to herself. She couldn't get over it. But it didn't matter, because there he was.

Osiris wasn't allowed to babysit William. Neither was Claire. Michael was sometimes reluctant, but he agreed when he couldn't argue he needed rest for work. That was most often on the nights before his days off.

One Thursday, Michael made plans with Sheena, a girl he'd met in the parking lot of Chili's, where he and his friends gathered every now and then to talk out their plans for the evening. Magdalene and her mother were driving Claire to Fort Worth for a two-week stay at a camp for underdeveloped girls. Claire would swim with other girls, learn to sew and make her own food. She would make friends. She would develop. Everyone in the family pitched in to provide this for her, and her sister and mother felt it was extremely important that they see her off. She'd never stayed away for more than a night.

Osiris was nearly eighteen. He was a quiet kid, but wasn't trouble. Not really. Michael sat beside Osiris on the couch. They watched something in black and white with the volume turned low. William was sleeping. Michael had the phone in his palm in his lap. He had decided to call Sheena to cancel the date. Osiris laughed at the TV program. An overweight black man in a cowboy outfit wandered from side to side in a saloon. A lean cowboy tried to trip him, but slid on the puddle from a spilled beer. The overweight black man began to laugh and the other cowboys circled him. A brawl broke out and Osiris erupted into hearty laughter. Michael laughed a little too, to show his brother he was a good sport. He said,

"Osiris, you're settled in for the night, right? You're not going out? You don't have plans?"

Osiris shook his head.

"Well, the thing is, I *do*. I have plans. I've got a date, and does it make sense to you that you're not supposed to watch the baby?"

Osiris shook his head again.

"Mom thinks I can't do it."

"See, and that's because she won't *let* you do it. She won't know you can handle it until you've *proven* you can handle it."

"How do I do that?"

"By watching William tonight. Just for an hour."

"You're watching William tonight."

"That's true. They asked me to."

They sat together a little longer, watched the show progress into a love scene. The main character sat outside a young woman's window, watched her brush her hair. She seemed to be singing, but the volume was too low to pick any of it out.

"He loves her," said Osiris.

"Have you ever been in love, Osiris?"

Osiris didn't take his eyes from the TV screen. He laughed a little.

"Probably not," said Michael. "I'm supposed to meet a girl tonight."

The main character slid off his horse, crept closer to the window. He was right below the windowsill and the woman put her brush down, leaned out the window and over the hero. She appeared to sing, full volume into the evening, and the hero was riveted. His hands were shaking, his feet tapping. He reached up, grabbed her by the shoulders and pulled her down to him. She immediately began to hit him up and down, all over his body. Across the arms and the face and he took every blow until she wore out and paused to see who she was striking, who was allowing her to pummel him so. It was the stableboy, the man she thought she would never see again. She fell into his arms and they held one another. The scene faded to black.

"What does she look like?" asked Osiris.

"Who?"

"The girl."

"Who? Sheena? She looks like . . . she looks Italian, I guess."

"Like her?" Osiris pointed to the heroine, who was now in a dimly lit apple orchard, plucking apples from a tree barely within her reach.

"Sure," said Michael. "I guess. Sort of like her."

They watched the movie a little longer, then Michael got up.

"You're going to be alright?" he asked.

"I'm alright," said Osiris.

"You're going to mind after William? Feed him if he's hungry? Walk him around if he's crying?"

Osiris nodded, watched the TV. Michael left.

After the movie was over, Osiris headed into William's room. The baby was sleeping on his back, head to the side. He moved his hand a little. Drool came out. Osiris leaned against the bars of the cage. They bent beneath his weight. His breath came hot and heavy over the baby while it slept. The baby had fat little legs. Its legs looked too fat for its pants. The fat bubbled out over the hem of his shorts. Osiris reached in, pinched the baby on the inside of its thigh. Nothing happened. He pinched a little harder and the baby squirmed. William brought his arm down, his leg up. His face puckered and he began to cry. Osiris pinched again, and the baby screamed. Osiris reached in and lifted his younger brother into his arms. The baby cried and cried in his arms and Osiris bounced him and spun his way down the hall whispering, *shhh*, until finally the baby got quiet again. Osiris placed the baby back in its bed and watched it move around. He lifted a small stuffed ball to his mouth, pressed it against his gums. Osiris sneezed onto the baby and he started crying again, bawling, and Osiris lifted him again, but this made the baby cry harder. Osiris bounced the baby and spun the baby and sang songs into the baby's ears but it did no good. Osiris played the record his mother had left in the player and when the music kicked up, William finally settled down. He pressed into Osiris' shoulder as he spun and bounced the baby, singing along.

Two hours later, Magdalene and her mother arrived. Michael was nowhere to be seen. Osiris had William in his lap on the couch. A war show was on and the men were talking about how your unit becomes your friends and your friends become your family. You're at war with your whole family and one day the bullets rain in and two-thirds of your family is cut down and you're surrounded by dead men you love but never really knew and Osiris was crying a little but held it back when his mother walked in.

"Where's Michael?" she asked.

"He had to step out," said Osiris. "He'll be back."

"That son of a bitch," said Magdalene. She scooped up William and asked him over and over again if he was alright. The baby burbled and she said, "You're alright. You're alright."

The next morning Osiris climbed on top of the house. Everyone except for Magdalene was asleep, but they were one after the other roused from sleep by the heavy clomping of Osiris's booted feet. Magdalene went out first, William in arm, to investigate the sound, and there was Osiris, on the roof, his arms spread wide like a goose in flight.

"Bring me the baby," he said.

"You're out of your mind," Magdalene said. She went inside.

"Who's on the roof?" asked their mother.

"Osiris is out of his mind," said Magdalene.

"Sy's on the roof?" said Michael.

"Come on down, buddy." Michael held one hand at his eyes to shield them from the sun, the other was at his hip. He was shirtless, in shorts. "Come down from there."

"I'm going to jump because no one trusts me," said Osiris.

"You're not going to jump, Sy."

"I am going to jump."

"You're not going to jump because if you jump, and you survive, I'll break your legs."

"Get down," said their mother. She tightened her robe and stepped down from the porch. "Listen to your brother. You're upsetting Claire and the baby."

"What about Maggie?"

"You're upsetting Maggie too, now get down."

"Bring me William."

"We're not bringing the baby on the roof, Sy. Get the hell down from there."

"I'm not getting down," said Osiris. "I'm jumping down."

"Sy, it's a fifteen-foot jump. If you jump, you'll just sprain an ankle. Get the hell down from there."

Osiris leapt. He landed on his face, his chest, his knees, toes, and wrists. He broke a wrist and bruised his face.

"No one trusts me," he told the doctor.

The doctor stretched his mouth against his teeth and shone a light in Osiris's eyes.

"Stop jumping from rooftops. Might be a step in the right direction." The doctor touched his knee and rose up. He smiled, said goodbye, and let Osiris's mother in. She drove him home in silence.

At the house, she stopped him in the hall. She hit him once and asked him if he knew how much this was going to cost them. He shook his head.

"You didn't think about it, did you? We're paying for this bullshit. Your little bullshit, we're paying for it."

He shook his head.

"You think we're not paying for it? You think it's free?" She raised her hand to hit him again, but stopped herself. She brought her hand down.

He shook his head. He was crying a little. She slapped the broken wrist.

"You shit." She left him there leaning against the wall.

The next morning everyone was gathered around the kitchen table.

"We're not sending him to a home," Michael said.

"We're not keeping him here," said Magdalene. "Not with William around. Not with you leaving them alone together we're not."

"Are you blaming me?"

"Someone put all this in his head."

"If you put even the slightest bit of faith in him . . . "

"Then what? Then what, Michael? He would have flown?"

Claire laughed at that, though Magdalene was yelling and the baby was crying.

They visited Osiris once a month as a group. They convinced him the facility was in his best interests. No one wanted to see him go, they said, but they wanted him to get better. They wanted him to be able to spend more time with William. They wanted William to grow up around an older brother who was safe and secure and happy. They didn't want William to grow up around a brother who was jumping off rooftops. The facility was more than they could afford and Michael took on a second job as night manager at a Dairy Queen. Magdalene got Claire a job at the Sonic. She still knew a few people. Claire refused to wear the skates. She got few tips. She made few friends. Customers complained about her attitude, her clothing stains, how often and how badly she screwed up the orders. Claire ate on the job. She spilled food on the floor purposefully so she could eat what they would otherwise throw away. She took smoke breaks, though she didn't smoke. During those breaks, she sat on her hand at the picnic table behind the building. She dug her hand past the loose belt around her waist, the elastic of her underwear. She farted on her hand and sat there for the full ten minutes. She did not offer service with a smile.

"You're going to get fired," Osiris said. They were gathered together around a circular table. He was all in white. "If they catch on to how little you care, they're going to fire you."

"Maybe," Claire said.

Their mother was at the vending machine, trying to buy five ice creams. The machine took her dollar in, whirred, and spat it out. She tried again.

"You need to give a shit," Magdalene said. She took out her breast, drew William to it.

"You're doing that here?" Michael said.

"Everyone's getting ice cream. Why can't he eat?"

"That baby is nearly a year old, Maggie."

"He likes it."

"It's disgusting."

"Shut the fuck up, Michael, and go have your own kid."

"Goddamn this piece of shit. Does anyone have a dollar?" Their mother was sweating, her sunglasses atop her head. "Do any of you have a dollar?" None of them did. Their mother was in possession of nearly every penny they earned. "Well, then I'll go without, I guess." She passed an ice cream to Michael, Osiris, Claire, and Magdalene.

"We'll split, Mom." Osiris broke the sandwich in half.

"You're my sweet boy," she said. She licked the sides first, brought the edges of the cookie together. "Mama's sweet boy."

"I wish Dad could be here." Osiris looked to the grated window, there was nothing to see. Michael watched his brother turn.

"What are you looking at?"

Their mother said nothing.

"If Dad was here," Osiris said, "this would be our TV moment."

William coughed. A dribble of milk fell to the curve of Magdalene's shirt, unbuttoned and hanging.

"I love you five very much," said their mother.

"We love you, Mom," said Michael.

"Yeah," said Osiris.

Claire nodded, finished her ice cream sandwich.

Magdalene said she loved her more than anything in the whole entire world.

They felt the room expand around them, as if someone were watching them, and had just taken a step back. The rest of the people in the room felt very far away, distant and indistinct.

"Here's to Raul," said their mother. She closed her mouth around the final bite of the ice cream sandwich.

"Here's to William," she said, and wiped her mouth.

William grew and grew. In grade school, he was the tallest kid in his class by several inches. He had thick arms, even as a boy. By middle school, he was a quarterback. Michael taught him to toss a spiral in the backyard. Osiris was out of the facility. He was quieter than ever, but peaceful. Claire was fatter than ever. She had been fired from Sonic and found a job at a snow cone stand just down the road. She drank cups of the syrup when no one was looking. She brought them back to William and he took packets of the stuff on long runs. He was running in the mornings, working out in the evening. The boy was a machine. They'd never seen anything like it.

"His father was pretty hunky if I recall," Magdalene said to her mother one afternoon. They were watching the boy climb a tree in the backyard. He climbed until the branches grew thin, dropped down and climbed again. Magdalene's mother laughed and batted her hand.

William never knew his father. His mother had grown up without a father too, and he had two uncles who wouldn't leave him alone, so he didn't think about it much. He wrestled with Osiris, played games with Michael. Michael was managing the hardware store where he worked and was taking night classes. He was exhausted most of the time, but loved watching William get worked up. Magdalene and her mother took up smoking together. They drank in the afternoons and watched their boys play and wrestle and they felt genuinely happy and content. They plumped up together. Claire bloated. Osiris chubbed up as well. Michael stayed lean and muscular and William was bursting at the seams. His veins were piano wire.

William and Michael drank beers on the back porch after dark. Osiris sat with them sometimes, but he never touched the stuff.

"You really jumped off the roof?" asked William.

Michael lifted his eyebrow, looked to Osiris.

"I did," said Osiris. "I wouldn't recommend it."

Michael laughed and Osiris laughed a little too. William watched them both. He wanted to understand his uncles, but there was something off about them. He never felt quite at home with them, but he enjoyed himself nonetheless. There was something missing, but he didn't know what. He'd never known anything but this, so he had nothing to measure it against. He asked for another beer and Osiris served him from the cooler underneath him.

"What was your dad like?" William asked.

"He was great," Osiris said.

"We didn't know him that well," said Michael.

"Dad was a hero," Osiris said.

"That's true," said Michael. "He was that."

The next morning, the television was gone. The front door was open. Mud streaked the carpet. Michael called the police and they came and filed a report.

"Let us know if you find anything out," they said.

The day after that, the rainy-day money was gone. Their mother kept a curl of bills in a coffee can in her sock drawer. She'd gone in to file away a quarter of Claire's paycheck from the snow cone stand, but the can was missing. She'd burst into Osiris's room and demanded he return the money, but he insisted he had nothing, knew nothing of what she was talking about. Michael asked him once, in private, if he'd seen the money, maybe noticed it out of place somewhere, which made Osiris cry and insist further he didn't know what they were talking about.

"Maggie?" asked their mother.

"Fuck you," Magdalene said. She left the room.

William came home from school to find everyone in a rough mood. Osiris had locked himself in the room he shared with William. Michael was in the backyard, smoking and drinking beer and working on the lawn mower. Magdalene was splitting a piecrust with Claire, who was sweating in a tank top opposite her sister. Their mother was on the phone with the police.

"That's twice this week," she said. "It's an epidemic. What are you going to do about it? What am I supposed to do about it? We can't live like this! Don't you think I've thought of . . . "

She saw William, smiled at the boy, and left the kitchen for the laundry room, closed the cord in the door.

"What's going on?"

"We got robbed," said Claire.

"I know."

"Again."

William didn't tell anyone, but he stayed up the entire night the night after the second theft. He waited until everyone fell asleep. He closed his eyes while Osiris rocked himself to sleep in the bed across from him, and he left the room. He set himself up in a chair in the living room, across from the door. The hours passed. He watched. He imagined all the great things he could do. The door opened and a masked stranger walked in. He grabbed the guy by his throat, body slammed him. Crushed his neck with his foot. The door opened, a masked stranger leapt in. There was no one in the room. William dropped onto him from above. He broke his neck in three places. He dragged the corpse out onto the lawn and pierced it through with a stake. He stabbed the stake into the ground and stood back. A masked bad guy entered the house through a window. William broke the window and shut it before the guy got his leg through, and William chopped the leg clean off. He dragged the one-legged crook into the living room and kicked him to death in front of Magdalene, Claire, his grandmother, and Michael. Osiris guarded the backdoor. A masked bad guy entered the house to find no one in it. There was nothing to steal either. The house was an empty shell. A hollow façade. He turned to leave, but William slammed the door, bolted it. He lit the oily rags and the house erupted into flames around the bad guy. The bad guy pressed his face to the glass windows in the living room, but he hadn't the strength to break the glass. He begged for his life, but William was unmoved. The bad guy collapsed into the flames and was consumed. They collected the insurance money and William built them a nicer, two-story house atop the ashes of their old house and the bad guy who'd tried to mess with them. He imagined all the great things he could do, and the sun rose behind him and his mother woke to find him asleep on a wooden chair across from the door.

She nudged him awake.

"Do you want breakfast?"

He nodded.

"Do you think violence is good?" he asked.

Magdalene broke an egg into a bowl.

"What do you mean?"

"I mean to protect yourself. Or people you love?"

"Do I think it's *good?*" She broke a second egg.

"Yeah."

"Yes. To protect yourself and your family. Yes, I do."

"And people you love."

"Do you love someone?"

"Sure."

"Someone outside the family." A third.

"No."

"Who do you love?" She whisked the three eggs in a bowl with milk.

"No one."

"Who do you *like*, then?"

"You make it sound like there should only be one." William sat up in his seat, looked away from his mother pouring eggs and milk into the pan.

"Oh ho, I see. Well, give me the list. Is Sheila on there?"

"Sheila?"

"The girl I saw you with the other day. The girl who walked you home."

"She's in seventh grade, Mom."

"Okay."

"That's a year below me."

"I'm well aware."

"Eighth graders don't date seventh graders, Mom."

"My apologies," she said.

"Unless you just want to score."

Magdalene laughed, poked the edge of the omelet, and then looked very sad.

"Are you scoring?" she asked.

William shrugged.

"Are you trying to score?"

"Mom."

"I should know these things. You can tell me."

"I just said I was just trying to score."

"You didn't say that," she said. She flipped the eggs.

"More or less, I did."

"Okay. You know I love you, right?" she said.

"Mom, yes."

"And you know I couldn't be happier with you, right?"

"Yes, Mom."

"Well, it was a very significant struggle having you, William. Our family wasn't ready. *I* wasn't ready. It was very hard."

"Okay."

"I'm just saying make sure you're ready is all." She slid the eggs onto a plate, cut them in half and gave them to William with a fork. "Orange juice?"

"How do I know I'm ready?"

"When you start to feel it, wait two years. If you still feel it, you're ready."

He ate the eggs. She watched. Two weeks later, there was another break-in. They put tape over Claire's mouth and molested her in her bed. They held her down. They poured gasoline on her. They weren't there to rob anyone. They lit a match. They'd been caught the month before. They'd robbed a liquor store in Sanger and accidentally killed the clerk. They were out on bail, awaiting trial. They dropped the match. She had no money. They trashed her room. They tore up books, shredded clothes, the sheets. One punted her goldfish in its bowl. It hit the wall with a thud, fell to the ground and spilled. The house burned around them. They climbed over her in her bed and kicked open the window against which the bed frame rested. They climbed out into the night to escape the smoke. The goldfish flipped, flipped again.

William's theory with gun shows was that you always brought a gun.

"There's no telling what kind of maniacs are walking around those places armed," he'd say.

He preferred pistols. He liked knives. Close-range weapons.

He worked at the local high school, as an art teacher. He enjoyed metalworking, bas-relief. He wrote spiritual poetry, which he called *sermons*. His girlfriend was a marathon runner.

He was at a gun show when the hospital called to tell him she had water poisoning. So he wound up bringing a pistol downtown, to the hospital nearest where she had finished the race. She hadn't stayed hydrated during the race and when she finished, she drank and she drank and she drank and collapsed. William brought his pistol into the back room of the emergency room and leaned in to kiss his girlfriend, who was sleeping.

"Love you, sweetheart," he said, and he left to go find balloons or flowers or something before she came to.

When he came back, a stuffed dragon under one arm, she'd switched rooms. He wandered the halls looking for her and before he found her, he happened across a room around which a large number of people were gathered. A line had even formed at the door, and people of all ages were going in and out, their heads hung low.

"Who's in there?" he asked a passing nurse. She shrugged. William got in line, if only to stand on his toes and see into the room. There was an elderly man in a bed there, and people gathered around him. He was talking to each of them, one after the other. He held their hands, kissed their palms. A few of the women were crying, a few of the men. William was moving forward in the line. Were these friends? Family? Was this a celebrity? If he got inside and the man spoke to him, what would he say? William inched forward until finally he entered the room. He took a spot by the old man in the bed. He needed to be by his girlfriend's side, not this stranger's, but it had all happened very fast.

"Father," said the man beside him, "I feel lost. I feel that life is too much for me. My kids are growing up. My wife is . . . she's not the woman I married." The man's head hung low.

"You must learn to appreciate what you have," said the old man. He took the other man's hand in his. "This moment. The unpredictable next. These are worth more than any dream you might have, any fantasy about what you could be doing or should be doing. A life-force moves through you, pulls you along, and you are me before you know it. And you will die."

It was William's turn next. The old man turned to him. His face curled up a bit.

"You're a new face." He shifted in his bed, placed his hands on either side of his frail body and pushed it higher up against the pillow behind him. "Are you a cousin?"

William nodded.

"I'm glad you came," said the old man. He took William's hand in his, held it. He closed his eyes.

William sensed he was about to move on, to greet the woman beside him. William did not want him to break contact. There was something extremely comforting in the man's kindness, his small body, his weak state. The man was so far from threatening. He was a spider web, the loose thread at the hem of a shirt. The man was next to nothing with his hands on William's.

"I, um, I brought you this," said William. He withdrew his hands and brought the stuffed dragon out from under his arm.

"Why thank you." The old man held the dragon out before him. "A dragon," he said.

William left. He found his girlfriend's room, in another hall. She was asleep when he entered. She was to be released in the morning. They wouldn't allow him to stay the night.

William went back to the gun show. There were a few more hours left, but people were packing their booths up early. He caught two men as they folded the long table that had held their literature on a new scope for William's preferred pistol. He talked them into giving him a few discount codes for their website.

He sat in the backyard with a BB gun for the rest of the evening, shot cans lined up along the fence. He loaded the gun, pumped until it was painful to push, and fired. The cans went flying. He drank beers and loaded the gun. A stray dog was sniffing one of the dropped cans. William pumped the gun. A car passed in front of the house and the dog moved away from the can, toward the field that opened up out of William's backyard. It was state land, marked off with a barbed-wire fence, but it was an old fence. The dog slid through and William watched it go. He went to the garage and found a shovel. He dug for an hour or so, a ditch in the backyard. He climbed inside. About knee deep and a few feet wide. He dug a little more because it felt good on his arms. The next morning he had to work. The ditch was a little deeper now. He climbed inside. He knelt and examined the mud walls. The end of an earthworm dangled there and he plucked it with his fingers, broke it loose from its front and brought it to his eye. The earthworm worked all the time. Or it never worked. He pressed his fingers together, smeared the earthworm between them.

His girlfriend's mother picked her up in the morning. William went to work.

When he got home, he had several messages on his answering machine. One was from his uncle Osiris. His cat was sick, needed medication and fluids daily. The doctor had once given the cat three weeks, but Osiris kept it alive for another two years. The phone call was an update on the cat's behavior. She was moodier than usual. She wasn't eating much. He was worried. The next message was from William's mother. He skipped it. The next was an automated voice. He let it play out while he scrubbed the cups and the bowls in the sink. He pried the dried food loose with his fingernails. The voicemail ended. His girlfriend clicked on. She was feeling better. The whole thing was terrifying. She'd thought she was going to die. She could have died. You don't get many second chances in life. She kept on like that for a few minutes, until she said she was ready to move on. She and William had been growing apart for some time now. She was pregnant. She didn't want any help. She hung up.

William had a drink. He called Osiris and let him talk about the cat for nearly an hour. William drank. What was left of the day dimmed. Osiris asked him to come visit and William said that, yeah, he might do that.

James made William call him Rad. He lived in a trailer at the top of a hill beside one of the busier country roads. He had built a little porch for himself, out of the back of the trailer, facing the hills. There was cattle land in one direction, country roads and a highway in the other.

"Babies are like these little worms that crawl out of them and started wriggling around and growing and they shit out a few other worms of their own along the way before they crawl into the ground and fall apart there." Rad loaded the skeet shooter and looked to William.

"Pull," said William.

He pulled the trigger and the disc shattered. Flakes of clay fell and William released his body into the lawn chair.

"See," Rad said. "I told you you'd feel better."

"I'd like to do something for them still," said William.

"She doesn't want any help, Will." Rad loaded the launcher. He took the gun out of William's hand and broke the neck. He popped the empty shells and loaded two more from his pocket. He placed the empty shells in the twelve-pack at his feet, half-empty itself. William crouched by the launcher.

"I know," he said.

He released the disc and Rad watched it fly. He turned slightly, matched the movement, got a lead, then fired. The disc disintegrated.

"Well," Rad said. "What did you have in mind?"

"I don't know," William said. "Money."

"Because what else would she want?"

William thought about the stuffed dragon. Maybe if he had brought her the stuffed dragon instead of giving it to that dying man who was probably dead right now. Maybe then he could have been there when the baby was born. Maybe then he could have . . .

"Your turn." Rad loaded the launcher. He handed the shotgun to William who propped it against his shoulder. He leaned forward in his chair.

"Are you still friends with that guy at the QT?"

"Randy, yeah."

"What kind of money on hand?"

"A thousand until eight. You're interested now?" Rad set the shotgun down on its butt.

"No," said William. He took the gun.

Rad loosed the disc and William fired. The disc soared on, arced toward the ground, and faded into the grass.

There were two men in the QT, other than Randy, when William pulled the pistol. He told them to get down, told Randy to keep his hands up. William climbed over the counter and had Randy open the register. One of the men rose up and fired on the two of them. Randy fell. William fired back, landed two in the man's chest. The other man covered his head and stared into the linoleum. William climbed over the counter and checked the man's pulse. Randy pressed a silent alarm. William found a spot of blood on his shirt, so he removed it, tore open the clear packaging that held a T-shirt boasting the colors and emblem of a local sports team. He put on the new shirt, grabbed a handful of cash from the drawer, and exited. He hadn't thought it through. Things hadn't gone right. He walked to the corner, where there was a bus stop. He waited only a few minutes, climbed onto the bus when it arrived. It held to the curb a moment, waiting for the police cars to pass before it could continue.

William rode the bus for about an hour. He got out under an overpass, and walked around to the stairs leading to the walking path that led out of town, into the next. He walked a few miles, an hour or so, and stopped when he saw a motel. He crossed the highway, crossed the access road, entered the motel sweating and panting and asked the man behind the thick glass if they took cash.

William collapsed into his stiff bed. The springs coiled into him. He emptied his pockets, counted the money. A couple hundred. A week or so.

In the morning, he left the motel. He walked a few miles in the heat, stopped at a restaurant. He ordered three tacos and a plate of rice and beans. He scooped the rice and beans into his mouth with the tacos, wiped his fingers across the plate, and left. Once outside, he jogged a little down the street, ducked behind another restaurant. He followed the path there through to the other side of the street, poked his head out, looked both ways, and continued on into the trees. Beyond the main drag of this town, there was the country. A few houses dotted the landscape, but he kept his distance from them, moved through the fields, stopped every now and then at a tree for shade.

For the first time in his life, William was totally alone. It was exciting, if not terrifying. He would need some money. That was the first order of business. And then some clothes. Eventually, food. He kept on through the fields until he hit a road. He chose left and headed that way. Cars passed, but he didn't hitch. There was no way of telling who was driving and he didn't want to take any unnecessary chances. It wasn't exactly safe, following a main road, but he needed to get into town somewhere, somehow. He needed to put together some money, maybe find a place to crash for the night. The first thing he came across was a gas station, but he walked right past it. Next, a grocery store. It was early afternoon at that point. A woman was wheeling her groceries out to the car in a cart and he offered to help.

"No, thank you, I'll be just fine," she said. She kept on, a little faster now.

He leaned against one of the bigger cars in the lot, shielded himself from the sun and from the view of the entrance. How did people make quick money in this town? He eyed a couple counting change in their car.

"You two looking to make a buck?" he asked.

They weren't.

William started checking doors. He tested five locked cars before one gave. He climbed into a champagne minivan, checked the dash and between the front seats for stored cash. Nothing. He checked the driver's side panel and found a pack of cigarettes. He didn't smoke, tossed them. He climbed into the backseat and waited. An elderly man opened the trunk of the van and loaded his groceries. William was curled in the backseat, still as he could be. The old man climbed into the front seat and started the car. He reached for his cigarettes and William sat up. William told the man he had a gun, to be still, to empty his pockets. The old man shifted in his seat. He pulled his wallet out, dropped it. His arms were shaking. He was making soft sounds with his mouth. William told him to get the wallet. He leaned over, sat back up and shot William in the face.

The old man called the police from a stranger's cell phone. He'd almost forgotten the gun was there. The gun had seemed to pull itself out. He'd only turned. Then the criminal's face had peeled back. His ears were ringing. He couldn't hear the operator's questions. The police came and took his information. They matched William's gun to the gun that shot the clerk back at the QT. They phoned William's mother. She sent his uncle.

Osiris showed up at the morgue nearly an hour and a half late. His feet were taped. He had on a knee brace.

"When I walk," he explained, "my knee turns slightly to the right. I can feel it with every step. Anyway, it's been getting sore. So I wear the brace. The brace clicks. It disturbs the cat. So I tape it. I tape the other one, or else my walk is off."

The guy at the morgue asked Osiris if he was ready to identify the body.

There was little to identify. His face was cleared from the eyes down. His mouth, gone. A tooth or two clung here and there, as if weeded through. The body had William's eyes, though. William's hair.

"That's him," said Osiris. "He was supposed to come over yesterday and he never came over. My cat gets nervous when I'm having visitors. I try to clean up a little bit and that makes her nervous. So I didn't clean for him. I was feeling guilty today about it, because my cat seemed nervous anyway. Maybe she can just tell when someone's coming over. Or when I think someone is coming over. Because he never came. My mom says I should put her down. But there's enough cruelty in the world without us going out of our way to kill our pets."

❧

William's daughter was born Mary Louise. Her grandmother and great aunt and uncles were not alerted to her birth. William's girlfriend, the marathon runner, moved in with her great-uncle Joseph and they went about raising Mary Louise. Joseph was an ex-army man. He received a pension. He was retired after forty-five years of work at Texas Instruments. Now he bought cars, fixed them up, and sold them. He walked everywhere he needed to go.

Mary Louise was a striking blonde from the day she was born. She had brilliant blue eyes like her daddy. Her mother talked to her about her daddy from time to time. She did not want to keep any secrets from the girl. She told her that her daddy had gone the wrong way, but she was bound to go the right way. Her daddy had been a good man, though. But good men didn't always stay good, that was one of the most important things she could ever learn. There were no guarantees. Everything changed in unpredictable ways, even the best things. Mary Louise needed to love what she had and be ready to let it go. Her mother loved her very much. That was the one exception to the rule. As long as she was living, Mary Louise would be her number one thing.

She sang to the baby, talked to the baby. The baby slept in her arms. Her great uncle Joseph, now Gran Joe, paced the kitchen. He put away dishes, swept the floor. He asked if they needed anything. They didn't. They rarely did. Or when they did they were sure to ask him. He rarely caught them in a quiet moment of need.

Mary Louise grew up alongside her mother and her Gran Joe. She learned to ask questions and she stopped her Gran Joe in his tracks one day when she looked up at him, past the arc of the hose he'd pointed in her direction, and said,

"Gran Joe, you're making me angry."

"She's an angel," said Gran Joe.

The men in Gran Joe's family had been military for as long as he had records. Generation after generation enlisted, were drafted, served. Never above a foot soldier, not one of them. Some of them died. Some lived and died later. He had letters from a few to their wives, mistresses, lovers. He sometimes read them to Mary Louise as bedtime stories.

Sweetheart, I'm thinking of you always. I hate to march. I complain about it every day. I complain often. The other men don't understand. You have always been sweet to me. You're my good listener. I miss how you listen. Love.

"Your great-great-grandfather was killed in combat by friendly fire," Gran Joe said.

"Is there a war going on right now, Gran Joe?"

"Not really," he said. "Not here. Not one you have to worry about." He kissed her on the head.

"One more?" she asked.

Darling, I wake each morning to thoughts of you. But they are bothered, pushed aside by the idea of my wife, your husband. Imagine if, when I return, we were rid of them. Imagine walking down the streets together, hand-in-hand,

and proud of it. Imagine the things we would say to one another in public. Imagine if you spilled your drink in front of the waiter, and we laughed and you were embarrassed and I could tell you I love you. Imagine how often I could tell you I love you. I would drown you in them. It is starting to rain. Each drop is a kiss from you. I am telling myself that. The ink is running, and I must go. I will make no great attempt to escape from the rain today, because I love you. I love you.

"This one was from a distant cousin of yours. He went to war to avoid cancer, survived the war, then died of cancer."

"How many people that you know have died?"

"Well, Mary Louise . . . most of them."

"We all have to die?"

"Yes."

"I have to die?"

"Yes."

"Not now?"

"Not now, and not tomorrow and not any time soon."

"Will you be there when I die?"

"I hope not."

"Will you read one more?"

"Gladly, Miss Louise."

Son, you're going to read this upon my death. Maybe months after, maybe only a few days. Maybe the war will be over, maybe it will never end. It feels end-

less. I feel sometimes like we're walking in circles. I'm writing because I think about you all the time. Not because I have anything in particular to say. Or maybe I have a few things to say, but it's not the kind of thing I thought I'd be putting in a letter. When you grow up, you're going to be handsome. You might not notice it at first. Girls will like you more than your friends and you might not notice that either.

Treat your friends well. They'll be around for longer. At least at first. Treat women well, too, I'm not saying you shouldn't. Treat them very well, but when you're young, you'll date more than a few, I'm sure, and most of them won't be worth the time it takes you to realize that. You'll have kids of your own one day. And they'll grow up fast. Life moves very fast. It's unbearable. Sometimes I look back over the things I've done, the things I've seen, even in the past year, and it seems one great big joke. Like nothing lasts even a moment. Just one thing then the next and it's all so fine and terrifying too.

War is a waste of time, son. If you can avoid it, do so. If you have to cut off your pinkie, do it. I would cut off my pinkie this instant if it meant I got to be back home with you and your mom tomorrow. In life, the best you can hope for is that you find something you love to watch change. I love watching you change. You and your mother. She used to have a different hair color, even. Her hair was blonde when I met her, not that I don't like the brown. But she was a blonde bombshell, that's the scientific term. She was the confidence I'd always lacked. She scooped me up and cut my hair and I was in love with her then and I'm even more in love now. I think about you two all the time. Every minute. It's an adventure out here, that's for sure. But I do not like it. It's an adventure back home, you'll see that soon enough.

Watch your friends, the paths they take. Watch the people around you and the way their lives change. Never fool yourself into thinking it's the same thing day after day, or else you'll wake up one morning and look back over your life and be struck suddenly with all the things you missed. You'll be in a strange place, you'll be a strange person. You'll have no sense of how you got where you are, what you're doing or why. Because you stopped paying attention. I stopped paying attention. Look at me now.

There are magnolia trees here. Would you believe it? Just like at home. Magnolias in bloom. Their leaves turn pink and drop into a circle around the base of their trunk. The men I'm with kick through the circles as we pass. The leaves lift, hold the air, and fall. You can press them with your boot, draw out a little bit of the liquid still in their veins. It leaves an oily streak wherever you *trace your foot. These are some of the small pleasures afforded us on a daily basis. Look for those, okay? When you can't find them, change something. Something drastic. Something you think you can't. I love you, son. I'll see you soon.*

"He shot himself in the leg."

Mary Louise was asleep, but she woke up, sat up.

"Put a bullet in his leg and was dishonorably discharged because everyone knew that he did it, and why he did it."

Mary Louise rubbed her eyes.

"He was your great-granduncle. My grandfather's brother."

"I want to meet them."

"Me too, sweetheart."

"I dreamed last night that I met the men in Gran Joe's letters," said Mary Louise.

Her mother poured apple juice into a plastic cup with a screw-top lid.

"I went to where you go when you die and met all of Gran Joe's family."

"What did they say?" asked her mother. She sat at the table where Mary Louise was finishing her pancakes.

"That I didn't have to die and be like them if I didn't want to." She picked up the last wedge of pancake and spun it on the end of her fork, twirling the syrup.

Gran Joe was in the other room, puttering around the television, the bookcase, the pile of toys.

"You certainly don't have to worry about it now," said her mother. Her mother folded the edge of the tablecloth in front of her.

Mary Louise dropped the wedge of pancake into the layer of syrup. Her mother stood, bent, touched her toes, and hung there for a minute.

"Did you stretch this morning?" she asked.

"I stretched," said Mary Louise.

"Did you finish your breakfast?" She rose up, vertebrae by vertebrae.

Mary Louise held out the last bite. "Want it?"

Her mother shook her head, sat on the floor and reached out to her feet.

Mary Louise grew up at an astonishing rate. She was tall, muscular like her father. She liked soccer, but didn't pursue organized sports after middle school. She went on runs with her mother, but tended to stop early. She dieted with her mother, but tended to cheat. Her mother had a schedule on the wall, an enormous calendar. Which foods when, how far to run, which parts of the body needed attention on which days. Gran Joe was always saying what beautiful, dedicated angels had flown into his life. He was healthy for an old-timer. He didn't smoke, didn't drink. Worked in the yard most of time. Mary Louise came home from a run and found him moving sticks around in the backyard. He followed her in, poured a glass of water, offered a bite of food. He was waiting for her, for her mother. He didn't do much else.

On weekdays, Mary Louise studied most of the night. At school, she told her friends she had a photographic memory. She debated. She took the advanced classes, did well in them. She decided she was going to be a poet. She sat under mesquite trees. She watched ticks climb the tall grass, hang from the tip of each blade. She noticed dogs taking naps, and how they sometimes yipped. Everything that came out of her was dark and painful to read. She wrote about blood and burning barns. She imagined miscarriages, leaned heavily on the imagery of the ticks. Women were birthing dead babies in the next town over. There was something in the water. She showed only one friend these early poems. He told her they were all great, each one better than the previous.

"You think so?" she said. It was morning. They met on the back porch, walked to school together. She plucked a dead mosquito from her coffee. "Like book-good?"

"Like anthology-good," he said. He was always encouraging her to go swimming. "What are you doing today?"

She shrugged. He was ditching, going to the lake.

At the lake Mary Louise spread out a towel like a blanket. She'd brought a bag full of books, and drew them out to her side. She read a little here and there, watched her friend swim, dive forward into the water. He encouraged her to get in, but she shook her head.

"At least get some sun," he said.

She was in jean shorts and a T-shirt. She removed the T-shirt and he gave her a thumbs-up. She wrote two poems in the margins of two books. She made a point of writing a poem whenever she had the opportunity. She firmly believed she was getting better with each poem. Maybe each poem wasn't better than the last, as her friend insisted, but she was learning new things, trying things out. Her hand moved more easily. She thought a little less. She was excited for the gap to close between thinking and writing. She was excited for the first poem she wouldn't have to make herself write, or at least think to write, think her way through. She was excited to channel something. She was excited for the muscle memory. Her friend lay beside her, on the side opposite the books.

"Sunscreen?" he asked.

She turned over, allowed him to press sunscreen into and around the strap of her bathing suit top. He paid special attention to the shoulders, to her sides, curled his fingers around to her abdomen.

"That tickles," she said.

He returned his hands to her back. With a subtle pinch, he unclipped the top of her suit. The strap split, fell to either side of her. She started to sit up and he ran his thumbs along either side of her spine.

"It's easier this way," he said. "Just stay down and it's all the same anyway. Did you write anything while I was swimming?"

"I started two new poems," she said.

"Will you read them to me?"

"They're not finished."

"I'd like to hear them," he said. He ran his oily hands along her arms, along her side. His fingers curled under, touched her sides, the sides of her breasts.

"Could you get my neck?" she asked.

He did. Her ears too. His hands went back to her sides.

"I'm never going to the lake again," she said.

"Why?" His hands paused.

"I'm reading," she said.

His hands resumed.

"Oh," he said. "Good start."

"I'm never going to the lake again," she said, "because sand is a precursor to glass, and glass is a precursor to those tiny cuts, the kind you get on the palms of your hands, the kind you don't notice until later, when your hands are full of blood. You curve your hands to catch the blood and they only fill faster."

His hands curled around to the sides of her breasts again. He extended his pointer finger on his right hand, fingered the edge of her nipple.

She turned.

"Watch it," she said.

He reached further until he was cupping her breast.

"Watch it," she said again. She rolled over, exposing her breasts for a brief moment before she lifted her top back into place and held it there with her hand. She dropped the book, pushed him away, and stood.

"Sorry," he said.

She clipped her top back on.

"What are you doing?"

"I'm sorry," he said. "I thought . . . "

She bent and lifted her T-shirt from the ground, slid it back on. Her toes curled and the sand collapsed around them. She felt a tremendous pressure on her chest. She felt angry, uncomfortable. She rolled her shoulders.

"How sorry?" she asked.

"I'm . . . I don't know, very sorry." He stood up, folded her towel and held it out to her.

She looked at her feet, the sand, at anything but him. She ignored the towel and he held it out for a moment before hugging it to his chest.

"Sorry enough to eat this?" she asked. She bent and retrieved a handful of sand, held it out to him.

"The sand?"

"Yeah," she said. "Are you willing to eat the sand so I'll forgive you?"

"You want me to eat the sand?"

She nodded. "Before it falls between my fingers."

"How?"

"With your mouth."

"All of it?"

"As much as you can get down. You have to really try."

"I'm not going to eat the sand," he said.

"Then I'm not going to forgive you."

"But I'm sorry," he said.

"Prove it."

"You're being mean for no reason," he said.

"For no reason?"

"A handful of sand because I touched a part of your breast?"

"If you eat the handful of sand, you can touch my entire breast. You can hold it."

" . . . "

"For fifteen seconds."

There were a few other families on the beach by the lake. Small children played in the shallow water. Parents watched from their towels. The day was still.

"In the car?" he asked.

"Wherever," she said.

"Do I have to eat that handful or can I get my own?"

"You have to eat *this* handful."

He held out his hands, cupped, pressed together. She held her hand over his palms and spread her fingers.

"Hold your hands together tight," she said. "If any spills, deal's off, and I'll hate you forever."

He was careful to make sure none of the sand spilled. He brought it to his mouth and poured about a quarter of it in. He chewed, swished it around.

"I need water," he coughed. A cloud of sand leapt out, drifted.

"Careful," she said. "Swallow."

He swallowed a little. He tried to swallow again, coughed. More sand escaped the open mouth.

"You're losing sand," she said.

"Uh cahn hehp it," he said.

She put her finger to her lips. She rolled up her sleeves. He swallowed a little bit more. He chewed, grimaced, swallowed. There was still a good amount of sand left.

He tried to swallow again, but erupted into a coughing fit. He curled his fingers to protect the remaining sand, but coughed out cloud after cloud. He choked a little, gargled a little. He bent over, spit into the sand in front of them. He spit clump after clump of sand at his feet.

"I can't," he said.

"Fuck you, then," she said. And she left.

Mary Louise had never hitchhiked before, but didn't hesitate to raise her thumb once she'd hit the highway. A truck pulled over almost immediately, about fifty feet ahead of her. The driver was middle aged and shirtless. He spat little squirts into a Dr. Pepper bottle he stored between his legs. Mary Louise climbed in.

"Where do you want to go?" the driver asked.

Mary Louise stared forward. It didn't matter. Away from the lake. Closer to town. She had a few more hours before it was safe to be seen wandering the streets of downtown.

"A few miles that way," she said. She pointed out the windshield. The driver pulled the truck into gear, turned back onto the road. Her swimsuit top was moist with sweat and rubbed a vague shadow into the white T-shirt over it.

"Coming from the lake?" he said. "Did you walk?"

She didn't say anything. Now that she'd had the time to think about it, she didn't think hitchhiking was the best idea. Accepting a ride from this guy was an even worse one.

"Do you like music?" he asked. She didn't respond, so he clicked on the radio. He turned the knob until a soft song fell into place. "Do you like country music?"

Nothing.

"That's okay," he said. He raised the bottle to his lips, squirted. "I didn't always like this kind of thing either. But you slow down after a while, can I say that? Can I offer you a bit of wisdom? I think I can. Or I can speak from experience. You slow down, and slower music starts making sense."

They rode on for another fifteen minutes without speaking. The music played. Song after song, the singers sang about loss and love, how to survive it all or simply that they had.

"You're very pretty," he said.

"This is fine," she said. It was a side of the road much like the one where he'd picked her up. She'd noticed they weren't exactly headed into town, though. She didn't know where they were headed, actually. She'd just pointed and he'd driven on. There were woods on either side of the road.

He pulled over, turned to her. "Here?"

"Yup." She got out, thanked him.

He watched her walk a bit in the direction from which they came. She turned into the woods, listened for the gravel scrape of his leaving. The car faded on its course. She wiped her eyes, walked deeper into the woods. Mosquitoes grew fat on her arms, the backs of her legs. Specks of mud popped as her sandals lifted. She walked deeper into the woods. She felt guilty of something, but she couldn't say what exactly. The sun was nearly half a day from setting. Skipping school, what had happened between her and her friend, how she'd responded, climbing into car with a stranger, abandoning that car out of a sudden fear, a sudden correction, too little too late maybe. But none of those reasons seemed the cause. She just didn't feel right. She felt heavy. Each step was a chore. She fought with Gran Joe every so often, over what should be done around the house. The fights didn't last long, though. She would push him, often by simple refusal, until he was just about to boil over, and he would leave the room, the house, the neighborhood. He'd never once yelled at her. Not once in her entire life. She wanted to see it happen.

She could walk back to the road. She could walk deeper into the woods. She had no sense of which would bring her home. The idea of hitchhiking was suddenly repellent. There were three people she could call, her friend, her mother, her Gran Joe. But it wasn't emergency enough yet to call any of them, to make the required admissions.

Night began to fall. The woods shrank around her. Trees were shorter and shorter. Their dry branches curved toward the other trees, mingled with them to form a brittle canopy. The earth cracked, flaked, flung dust at her ankles as she walked. She bent over to avoid the branches, as they grew closer to the ground. The branches reached down, nearly to the earth as she moved deeper into them, but on the other side, there was a lighter shade of blue, things seemed to thin out. She thought she heard the roar of a car every so often, coming from that direction. She was on her hands and knees all of a sudden, crawling over the caked earth. The branches snagged her hair, teased it out of the little clips that held it in place. Her sunglasses bounced against her chest. She was on her belly, dragging the lenses in the dust. She remembered the songs she'd heard in the cab of the truck. In one of them, the woman sang, *It ain't no problem, ain't no problem, no problem, the world is spinning. It ain't no problem, the world is spinning.* The gaps between the branches grew smaller. She crawled on her belly toward where the trees seemed to thin, where she would be able to stand, able to walk, able to brush herself off and let her palms sting the cuts along her arms and chest as she approached the road, with its heat waves and oil slicks, only a few feet away, and where she would be so immensely pleased with herself, as her feet met the asphalt like an old friend, and she would begin to walk in whatever direction felt right, while cars passed, and in the distance, she might discern the two waist-high headlights of an approaching truck.

Months passed, years, and the posters faded. Gran Joe posted new ones. He walked with a cane, stapled each new poster individually to billboards, random telephone poles. He turned them in at bookstores, coffee shops, pizza parlors. He called detectives, left messages. Mary Louise's mother ate birthday cakes topped with a variety of ice cream flavors. Mint chocolate chip, strawberry, birthday cake, peppermint, bubble gum, blackberry, rocky road, and plain old vanilla.

She gained weight. She brought home a man who liked "large women." His name was Cliff, and he had only a few teeth. He kept his fingernails long, liked to click them against his glass when he drank. He'd been a boxer once. He sat on the front porch with Gran Joe, and told him the stories of old matches. These conversations were painful for Gran Joe. His entire family had fought with purpose, and this man was doing it for sport. Gran Joe found reasons to leave for a moment, claimed he needed to use the restroom, asked if Cliff needed another beer. Gran Joe sat on the toilet, his pants at his ankles, and did nothing. He enjoyed the time to himself. He wanted to be alone. He wanted Mary Louise back.

When Cliff needed a place to stay, he turned to Mary Louise's mother. Gran Joe suggested the two of them, Cliff and his grandniece, find a place together. She seemed happy around him, or they seemed happy together. She laughed at least. Before, she'd slept most of the time. She'd taken Tylenol PM by the handful, drank Robitussin.

"I'm not saying you've got to leave," he told Mary Louise's mother. "But I can't have him living here."

She left. Their house was a tomb anyway. There were stacks of Missing posters, pictures everywhere of Mary Louise. It would be nice to start over. It would be nice to get out from under all the grief and quiet evenings. Cliff wanted children. He wanted to start a business. He was going to take care of her. Her life could be entirely different.

Cliff mowed lawns for a living. Twenty bucks an hour. He said he met interesting people this way, got to know the neighborhoods and spend most of his days outside. There were worse things he could be doing with his days, he said.

They were able to afford a small apartment on the edge of town. She found work at a 7-Eleven, as the night manager. He mowed during the day, drank during the evenings. She set her alarm an hour early, so they could have sex before he fell asleep and she needed to be at work.

Within three months at their new place, she was pregnant with twins. She named them Joseph and Cliff Jr. the day she found out. She drove home from the gynecologist's office, rubbing her stomach, singing to herself. *Not to myself*, she thought, *to Joseph and Cliff Jr.* She couldn't be happier that there would be two. They could watch out for each other and neither would ever get lost.

Cliff broke a lamp when he found out. He was shirtless and yelling and circling the open space in the living room. They didn't have money for two kids. He pushed her, pressed her against a wall.

"What am I supposed to do?" he said.

She couldn't breathe, not really. She couldn't say anything.

"Well?"

She thought to knee him in the groin. She thought to hit him in the mouth, claw out his eyes, hit him in the gut. She thought of choking him, stabbing him, drowning him in the puddle behind their apartment complex, thick with mosquito eggs.

She shook her head, looked around the room. She didn't fight. She gave in, went limp in his arms. He stepped back and she stuttered forward, regained her balance.

"I'm sorry," he said. He left the room, got a beer from the fridge, and sat down at the table.

Her blood was still hot. Her body was sore all over. While he drank, she found the gun he kept in his closet, a twenty-two he'd stolen from a neighbor's yard, years before.

"Right off the porch," he liked to say.

The television exploded and he was up and out of his seat. Beer spilled onto his legs and splashed against his bare chest.

"What the hell?"

He entered the living room and she had the gun against her collar bone, smoke at the barrel. The television spat a spark. She turned the gun on him, asked him to leave.

"That's my gun," he said.

"It was never your gun," she said.

She wrote Gran Joe for money. He sent checks, along with letters asking her to visit, asking if he could. She answered his letters, but never his questions. She talked about other things. She talked about work, about her body, what it was like, having two inside you instead of one. She didn't always send these letters. They were personal. He didn't push the issue of a visit, asked every few letters how she might feel about the idea. And she never replied.

She was starting over. This was something new. Cliff didn't matter, he never had. She changed Cliff Jr.'s name to Jimmi. Jimmi and Joseph. She liked the sound of that, for a set of twins.

She couldn't get comfortable in the apartment she'd shared with Cliff. It wasn't the right space to raise a set of boys, and she couldn't shake the feeling that Cliff was still there, in another room somewhere, on the toilet, drinking in the kitchen, behind the shower curtain. She found a carriage-house apartment behind the home of an old couple, married fifty-two years. They left her alone mostly, congratulated her on the boys. Every so often, the wife from the couple would bring her some of whatever they were having, a few slices of chicken in gravy, some mashed potatoes, some apple crisp. But she refused the food more often than not. She felt strong, like she was doing a good thing. The right thing. Her sons grew inside her. The checks from Gran Joe came biweekly. She worked at the 7-Eleven until she was seven months. Then she started accepting food whenever her landlord made the offer. It wasn't long before they offered to have her in. She ate with them at their small dinner table, in the middle of the kitchen. They sat back together, after the meal, considered one another. She felt like she filled the entire room. She imagined herself befriending them. She imagined their always wishing they'd had a daughter, seeing her as such. They would bring her into their house, feed her, love her, and when they died, they would leave her everything.

She imagined the old woman dying. The husband so stricken with grief that he asked her in for dinner, time and time again.

"You're very beautiful," he would say. "You are very, very beautiful."

At first, she would care for him. Feed him, keep his medications straight, cook, clean, that kind of thing. He would grow to depend on her, to love her, and he would ask her to marry him and she would say yes because when he died, he would leave her everything.

"Thank you," she said.

They nodded.

"We like to watch a movie after dinner," the old man said. "Or sometimes the TV. Would you like to join us?"

"Henry," said his wife. "She wants to sleep."

"Of course," said the man. "Forgive me." He took their plates.

"This was lovely," she said.

"Yes," said the old woman. She rose and went to the counter. She stood there for a moment, her hands hovering at the linoleum, then left for the living room. The television clicked on. The room filled with laughter.

The old man had his back to his tenant at the table. He wiped the plates with a flower print rag.

"Good night," she said.

He nodded. "Good night."

She applied to be a part of a program that would pay for her hospital bills when she had Jimmi and Joseph. She had to sign a paper that she imagined told her that she had no way of supporting herself, and never would.

The babies came. She was relieved. For a day or two, she was relieved. Then she started working out. She jumped rope in the center of the carriage house while the babies slept. She worked extra hours. Her landlords babysat a handful of times. She got money from the state. She worked. She put ads in the paper, online. She was looking for someone independent, with a comfortable living situation. She was looking for someone who was mature. Someone who knew what wine went with what. Someone who worked out. Someone who liked mothers. Someone with money. She was looking for someone with money.

She placed a T-shirt over the lap of one of the sleeping babies. She touched the nose of the other, his cheek.

"Jimmi," she said, pointing to the shirt. "That's *your* name."

He did not move when she tucked it between his legs and the car seat. The face of Jimi Hendrix moaned up at her.

"And Joe," she said. She followed the same procedure with the other child, securing the edges of a Joe Perry shirt between his limbs and the cushion of the car seat.

She got home early. There wasn't a soul on the road.

The babies slept on while she prepared dinner. The carrot skins slid off easily, with only a few strokes. The water boiled after only a moment. She had a small glass of wine. A strand of pasta stuck to the wall.

Perry arrived. He saw the babies, swaddled in the Jimi Hendrix T-shirt and the Joe Perry shirt, and he put on a record. She danced into the room, a second glass of wine in her hand.
"I made pasta," she said.

They made love on the living-room floor. She scuffed her knees on the carpet. Jimmi stirred. The pasta cooled. She told Perry not to stop when he was ready to come, not to slow down. He didn't. After, he slid down between her knees and she leaned over him, pressed her palms into the carpet. She made quiet sounds: the baby was only a few feet away. She glanced every now and then at the babies, checked to make sure they were sleeping, safe, as something moved through her, a scream of blood rounded the curves of each ear and her body seized, released, and Perry paused.

"Did you?"

She slapped the carpet and he began to move again, his fingers, his tongue, his chin. He pressed her with the tip of his nose. Joe stirred. She looked over once more, before she collapsed.

They lay together on the carpet, slick and smiling.

"Will that fuck him up?" Perry asked. He meant either.

She shrugged. She didn't think so. Their eyes had been closed the entire time; they'd held them tight, there in their chairs.

She and Perry ate the pasta naked. She dropped noodles onto her lap, between her legs and onto the chair.

"We need a dog," she said.

❁

They bought a dog for the babies, named it Sid.

"Sid's your dog," she explained.

Joe cupped his hands, held them up. Jimmi coughed some foam onto his lips, sucked it back in.

"One day you won't be able to imagine having lived without him. That's the way I feel about you."

Jimmi coughed again, a mess of white foam onto his cheeks, neck, and chest. She wiped it away with the hem of her shirt.

Joe and Jimmi grew up alongside Sid. Sid was big and black and the toddlers could ride him a few steps before sliding off. Perry held each of them, one at a time, on Sid's back until they slid and Perry cried, "Lift off!" and flew the toddler around the room in sweeping arcs and curves until bringing him down safely to land on the couch by his brother.

As a young boy, Jimmi spent a lot of time by the creek behind their house. He caught lizards and snakes and reptiles and showed them to Sid, who was almost always with him. Joe lost interest in Sid early on. When he pushed at Joe's legs at the table, Joe swatted at him and Jimmi told him to stop. Jimmi fed the dog bites of food with one hand, held his own bites with the other.

When Jimmi caught animals, he brought them home to show his mother and her boyfriend. Perry didn't live with them, but he was around all of the time. Perry had his own house. He drove a nice car that went faster than Jimmi was comfortable going. He didn't like riding with Perry in the car because Perry would rev the engine. He would say, "Listen to her, she wants it," and he would speed through lights, take corners too fast, and curse at the other drivers when they got in his way.

Sometimes Jimmi kept the animals he found. Most of the time, he let them go. His mother always made him choose his favorite one. He could keep that one for a week before letting it go. He had two frogs and one grass snake in his permanent collection. They had not left the porch when he placed them there after a week of taking care of them at home.

"They're spoiled," Perry had said.

"They love me," Jimmi had said.

"I'm sure they do. But I bet they also love their freedom."

When they were still there in the morning, Jimmi said, "They love me more than their freedom, Mom." And that was that. Jimmi became the proud owner of each brand-new pet.

Sid was always hungry. He slobbered on the carpet, on the porch, on Jimmi. Sid dipped his face into the creek, hung his cheeks just below the water as if to clean them. He watched the small fish with a keen eye. He did not pounce. He had never really pounced. He behaved as if he were born trained. He had sat and watched the two frogs and the grass snake on the porch. He cocked his head. They didn't move. There seemed an understanding between them. Jimmi said they were all his friends and his friends would not hurt one another.

It was summer. The heat was getting worse and worse. Their backyard was without trees, without shade, so they started keeping Sid in the house. One day, while Jimmi and Joe were at school, their mother at work, Sid knocked the cage containing the two frogs and the grass snake off the bookcase. It fell, at least. Perry discovered the mess, blamed the dog, but Jimmi insisted they had no way of knowing what really happened. The frogs and the grass snake were gone, though. The tank lay shattered on the carpet in Joe and Jimmi's room, a splatter of dark brown where the water had soaked in. Crickets leapt around the room, under the doors and into the kitchen.

"You have to clean it up," Joe said. He turned on the television, opened a math book at his lap. He set down his pencil.

Jimmi brought Sid outside. He looked him in his eyes. Sid's mouth ran. Saliva streamed from his sagging cheeks. He would not look at Jimmi. He would not sit still.

Jimmi gripped the collar and forced Sid to look at him.

"Did you eat the frogs and the snake?"

Sid couldn't answer. He didn't understand the question. Jimmi could tell just by looking at him. Why were dogs so stupid?

"Why are dogs so stupid?"

Jimmi's mother was drinking wine and leafing through a magazine at the kitchen table.

"They don't have access to the same opportunities as you," she said. "Oh." She put her hand to her mouth, looked around the room for someone who could appreciate her joke.

"Sid's a stupid dog," Jimmi said. "I think he was born stupid. I think I hate stupid dogs."

"Sid's not stupid, sweetie," she said. "He's just a dog, and dogs don't think like humans think. He might be very smart for a dog."

"He's an idiot," Jimmi said. He kicked the kitchen wall and left the room. He walked past the broom Joe had set out for him in the hall, over the glass on the floor in his bedroom, and climbed into bed.

In the morning, Jimmi woke up earlier than his mother or brother. He went out back, where they had chained Sid. He unclipped Sid's collar from the lead. He unhitched the back fence, opened it wide. There was a field behind the house. It led down to the creek he liked to explore. The creek he used to explore with Sid.

"Go," he said.

Sid sat.

"Get," Jimmi said.

The dog collapsed onto his paws. His tongue fell out. It was slick and shining and foamy.

"You're the worst dog ever," Jimmi said.

Sid slobbered onto the grass. Then he ate the slobber and the grass.

Jimmi went inside and got a plate of leftovers from the fridge. He placed it on the other side of the fence.

"Eat," he said. "Eat this."

The dog got up. He went over to Jimmi, sniffed his hands, licked them, then lowered his head to the plate. Jimmi closed the fence and hitched it. He had to push Sid's butt slightly to get the fence fully closed. The dog had looked up, but only for a moment. He went back to eating. It was spinach quiche, marbled with thick streams of green. Jimmi knew Sid would like it.

"Have you seen Sid?" his mother asked, later that morning.

"Nope," said Jimmi.

Perry hung a few signs on telephone poles around town: MISSING LAB. But they heard nothing. Jimmi told his mother he asked people on the street, told them he'd gone to the grocery stores, to the neighbors. No one knew anything.

After a month of searching, they had a mock funeral in the backyard. Perry dug a hole, where he placed what was left of the dog food. He said it seemed like a waste. Jimmi's mother was openly weeping. Joe dug his toe into the dirt at his feet. He looked around. They gathered together around the hole. Had a moment of silence. They watched two movies that night. A cartoon, and an action movie Perry had chosen. In it, a detective found his girlfriend's dog skinned and hung from a doorframe in his apartment. Perry laughed a little, which made Joe laugh hysterically.

"Quit it," said his mother.

Jimmi ate a handful of popcorn. He felt sad, but guessed he knew why they were laughing. The dead dog looked really fake. The detective was overacting. None of it seemed very real. His heart was racing. He ate another handful of popcorn.

No one wanted another dog. Sid had been their dog, and Sid was gone. Jimmi collected more snakes. He convinced his parents to let him keep them a little longer than a week sometimes. His room smelled like dead crickets and feces. Joe complained, lit candles. He demanded his own room and, eventually, their mother cleared her study of the boxes of photos and keepsakes she'd been storing there since she'd met Perry, since he'd moved them into this new home, an actual house, with actual rooms and two bathrooms, and their family had filled the extra space like a goldfish.

They grew up. All of Jimmi's frogs and most of the snakes died. One lived for ten years, until Jimmi and Joe started high school. It died one winter—Joe had unplugged the heat rock to make room for a guitar amp—and that was the last of the snakes.

Jimmi's mother was dressed in lace. It was the first time she had ever been entirely so. She looked elegant. She felt important, well shaped, soft, and worth touching. She felt like many people would want to touch her. Perry watched her from the bed. She fiddled with powders at the chest of drawers. They were new, and so was the lace. Perry bought her new things. They had no more money than before, but they were beginning to look as if they did. She was losing weight. She felt happier than she'd been for as long as she could remember. Her sons were growing up to be mature young men. She felt proud of the three of them, proud of what they'd accomplished. They were normal. That meant they had less to worry about in general. Life was stressful, but they did not have the added anxiety of an insecure position in the world. Perry worked. She worked too. Perry unbuttoned his pants, slid them down to his knees. His wife raised her head, but did not look over. She dabbed at her neck with a small brush, streaked a thick line of white powder, which she smoothed with her hand. He moved his hand along his thighs and watched her.

"Thank you," she said. She did not look away from the mirror.

With the palm of his hand, he encouraged his penis to lift.

"These." She pressed her lips together. "Are fantastic."

He curled his fingers.

"Come to bed," he said.

She turned to him, smiled.

"In a minute."

Joe and Jimmi were athletic, muscular, likeable. They did well in school. They were popular. People were attracted to them. Both men and women were drawn to them. People seemed to feel better around them, comfortable. The hallways brightened with their presence. Joe embraced this. He developed an enormous circle of friends. He knew nearly everyone in the school, in their hometown. People waved to him on the street. Jimmi kept to himself mostly. He was quiet, withdrawn, but he was still magnetic.

Jimmi had one close friend. He was small, bony. The friend admired Jimmi. He said yes to nearly everything Jimmi suggested. They ran together, explored together. They threw bricks through the windows at the Piggly Wiggly. They slashed the tires of strangers. They snuck into their neighbors' backyards, swam in their pools.

Jimmi went to the creek with his friend, threw trash from the creek bed into the water. He threw in a McDonald's cup. He threw in a chunk of metal.

"Do your parents still fuck?" Jimmi asked.

"Yeah," said his friend.

"How do you know?"

"I don't know. I can just tell. I think I've heard them."

His friend threw a Doritos bag. It was lifted by the wind, curled on a current, and then it landed back on the creek bed where they stood, only a few feet away.

"What did it sound like?"

Jimmi gathered a handful of rocks and went over to the bag. He dropped them in.

"Like a giraffe," he said. "Like a giraffe, I think. And maybe a dog or something. Like animals trying to move the furniture."

"Sick."

Jimmi threw the weighted Doritos bag at the water. It hit the surface with a smack. It sank. Bubbles rose to the surface and broke.

"Nice," said his friend.

Jimmi shrugged.

"You guys have nice furniture," he said, after a moment.

Jimmi shrugged again. There was very little garbage left where they were standing. Strips of plastic, paper adhered to rock. Nothing he could throw. Nothing that would sink.

"Does your dad have a big dick?" Jimmi said.

"I don't know."

"I bet he does," Jimmi said. "I bet he has a big dick."

Jimmi's friend said he didn't know. Jimmi's friend had only seen two dicks in real life. His and his father's. He had no way of knowing how either of them compared to the rest of the dicks in the world. He had no idea what was normal.

"Okay," Jimmi said. He lowered his pants. He spread his legs and swayed at his hips. "Ooh," he said. He pulled up his pants, threw a plastic bottle into the creek.

"Yeah," his friend said. "I think you're right. I think my dad has a huge dick."

While they thought Jimmi was at the creek, Perry went down on Jimmi's mother at the kitchen table. They had been drinking lemonade and he'd slid under the table like a lithe teenager. He parted her knees, pulled her underwear aside. She settled into her seat. She put down her glass and it clicked on the table.

She admired her children. How intensely they felt things. How dedicated and focused they could be. How they embraced their wants, their interests in a way that had seemed foreign to her for many years.

Jimmi's mother gripped her seat to steady herself. Perry was on his knees, focused, working, rhythmic, determined. She kept her eyes on the window. She closed them. She felt guilty, didn't know why. Condensation from the glass pearled along its side, grew heavy and fell. A ring gathered on the table. Her rings clicked the chair she held. Perry's neck cracked and she rose up slightly. He was growing a beard. She could feel it on her inner thigh. It tickled. It did not seem connected to him. Her rings clicked and she watched the window. A cluster of cicadas detonated and she felt blood inside of her, moving through her. Perry slowed.

"Did you?" he said.

She shook her chin, closed her eyes. He slid back under the table. Jimmi was at the backdoor, his face pressed against the window. He saw his mother squirm. Her eyes were closed. He knew what was happening but he did not know what was happening. He told his friend to go home, sat on the step at the door for what felt like hours. He pressed a beetle with his fingertip, popped it against the hot concrete.

"Are you having another baby?"

Jimmi found his mother on the couch, considering a basket full of laundry. She looked up.

"No." She cocked her head. "I don't think so."

"Good." Jimmi came around and sat on the couch with her, on the far side of the laundry basket.

"Why?"

"I don't think you should," he said.

"Why's that?"

"Babies are awful," he said. "They wet themselves. They cry. They can't do anything for themselves."

"You were a wonderful baby," she said. "I don't even remember you crying. I'm sure you did, but I don't remember it."

"Joe did all the crying?"

"Joe didn't cry either. You were both perfect babies," she said.

"Just don't have another baby, okay?"

"We won't," she said.

He didn't like the way she said *we*, like it was her and Perry against him.

"We won't anytime soon. But a baby would be a wonderful thing, Jimmi. Not a bad thing."

"It would be a pink wriggling thing that would pee and not take care of itself and be disgusting. They're disgusting, Mom."

"We—"

Jimmi knocked the basket of laundry onto the floor. Some fell out, but most clung to the bundle she'd made when pulling it all from the dryer.

"Jimmi," she said.

"Don't, okay?"

"Jimmi."

He left the room, kicked a small pile of socks. It tumbled once or twice then settled. She gathered the laundry back into the basket and brought it into the kitchen where Perry was drinking lemonade and reading the paper.

"What was that?" Perry said.

"He knocked the laundry over."

"That's it?"

"He said we shouldn't have another baby."

Perry smiled. "Smart kid."

One Sunday, Jimmi and his friend were checking dumpsters behind the Kmart.

"What are we looking for?" asked his friend.

"People drop babies in these things. We're looking for babies," Jimmi said.

"Gross." His friend lowered the lid of one dumpster, opened the next. "This one's full of books."

"What kind?"

"Says, 'The Gateway to Lucid Dreams'." Jimmi's friend held up one of the coverless books.

"Found it." Jimmi propped the plastic lid of the dumpster up with on hand, reached into its open mouth with the other. He pulled out a slick body, roughly the length of his forearm.

"Gross!" Jimmi's friend dropped the book. "Is it . . . ?"

"A baby," Jimmi said. "Someone left it here."

It was an opossum, a few days dead. Jimmi wrapped it in newspaper from the garbage. He carried it under his arm as they walked home.

"Let's throw it at a car," said his friend.

"Can't throw a baby at a car," Jimmi said. "We need to give it a proper burial."

His friend nodded.

"Let's throw it into the river," he said. "From the bridge. Let's put it on the railroad tracks."

When Jimmi and his friend got home, the front door was locked. No one answered when Jimmi knocked. Joe was out, he ran on Sundays, spent the rest of the day with his running friends and those that flocked to them as the day dragged on. Jimmi went around to the back of the house, the opossum under his arm. He stood on the AC unit at the side of the house, cracked one of his bedroom windows. He had long ago removed the screen for easy access. He slid through the window and lowered himself onto his desk. The opossum slid back and forth in the moist fold of his armpit. He felt its skin give to the pressure, glide, along with the muscle, against the bone.

"Let me in," said Jimmi's friend, from the window.

Jimmi opened his bedroom door and stepped into the hallway slowly, cautiously, the opossum sliding out from under his arm and behind him. Its tail worked its way out of the mouth of the bag, dangled there like the tiny tip of an off-white tongue.

His mother was on the living room floor. Perry was pushing her forward from behind. She was entirely nude. Perry, from the waist down. He had on a black T-shirt. Jimmi hurled the opossum and it struck the far window, bounced with a thud, and landed on the carpet beside them.

His mother fell onto her front. Perry lay upon her.

"Give us a moment," his mother said.

"What is that?" Perry pulled himself up. He stood over the opossum, his wet, erect penis glistening in the sun that leaked through the cracks in the mini blinds.

Jimmi's mother covered her face with her hands.

"We need a moment, Jimmi," his mother said.

Jimmi's friend tapped the window.

His mother reached for a cushion from the couch. Her fingers fell shy of its edge, fell to the carpet.

Perry stood over the opossum, looked back at Jimmi.

"What the fuck is this? What are you trying to pull here?" He brought his foot up over the opossum, pressed it down upon the rotten animal's bulging stomach. It popped, slung sludge onto the carpet, Perry's ankles. His calves were dotted with the mess. He turned his body, his glistening dick, toward Jimmi. "Well?"

"I'm sorry," Jimmi said.

"Sorry?" Perry brought his foot out of the dead rodent. He stepped toward Jimmi, tracking the sludge along the carpet as he did so. Jimmi stepped back. "Sorry for what?"

"Stop it, Perry." Jimmi's mother was pulling her clothes from a chair by the couch. She pulled on her shirt, her pants. She rubbed her hands against her head, pressed her hair down. "Stop."

"What's he sorry for?" Perry turned toward her. "What were you trying to do?"

"I . . . I don't know. You have to leave," Jimmi said.

"This is my house, Jimmi. You're a guest."

Perry was only a foot or so away from him now. Jimmi thought he could feel the heat of his body.

"Perry, get dressed. Let's talk about this."

"You're a spoiled shit," Perry said. He grabbed Jimmi's wrist and squeezed the veins just beneath his palm.

Jimmi resisted, tried to pull his arm away, but Perry held strong, stared him in his eyes.

Jimmi hit him. He hit him once across the mouth. Once against the back of his head.

"Jimmi."

Perry fell and Jimmi turned around, ran back to his room. His friend was still tapping at the window.

"Jimmi," he said. "What's going on?"

Jimmi exited through his bedroom window, climbed down the AC unit and past his friend, who followed him asking what had happened to the baby.

Jimmi led him to the creek. He took his shirt off, his shorts. He looked at his friend who asked again what had happened.

Jimmi climbed into the creek.

"You and I are going to get married," he told his friend. "We're going to be a new family."

Jimmi's friend just stared back at him. Jimmi was near nude, ankle deep in the creek. He stared at his friend like a bull. His friend removed his shirt, his shorts. He climbed into the creek, ankle deep.

They both waited a moment. The water broke against their ankles, moved past them. Jimmi took his friend's wrists.

"There," he said. "It's done."

When they came back later that evening, Perry was gone. Jimmi's mother was gone. Joe was in the living room with two girls, a blonde and a brunette. Jimmi told them he was leaving, moving in with his friend.

"You're doing what?" Joe said.

"I'm leaving. Alex and I are moving in together. Tell Mom we got married. Tell her, her gay son got married and is running off with his husband to go live anywhere other than here."

Jimmi threw a few shirts in a bag, some underwear. He didn't know what to bring. He didn't want to think about it. They weren't sure where they were going. It didn't matter.

"I didn't know you were gay," said Joe.

"Yeah, well."

And Jimmi left.

Jimmi and Alex drove late into the night. They stopped for gas. Jimmi bought cigarettes. They kept driving.

"What are we looking for?" Alex said.

Jimmi smoked.

"I didn't know you smoked."

"Yeah," Jimmi said. "Turn here."

Alex turned. He followed Jimmi's directions until they reached Oak Street, where Jimmi told him to stop alongside a dark-blue Mustang convertible. Jimmi got out of the car.

"Pop the trunk," he said.

Jimmi came out from behind the car, tire iron in hand, and struck the headlights of the convertible. He struck the hood. He shattered the windshield, each window. He popped the taillights, dented the hood. The alarm rang out. He struck the doors, the hood once more. He got back into Alex's car. They drove until sunrise. Alex talked. Jimmi smoked.

"That felt good," Jimmi said.

He kissed Alex. And after that, Alex wanted to hold his hand. Jimmi fiddled with the locks. He smoked. He changed the radio station, kept his hands busy.

"I need to stop at my house," Alex said. "I . . . I need to tell my parents I'm alright. We've been gone a long time."

"We can't do that," Jimmi said.

"But I've never been gone this long."

"One night?"

Alex shook his head. He tried to touch Jimmi's hand again. "Whatever, I'm staying in the car," said Jimmi.

Perry was waiting for them at Alex's house. His Mustang was there, its bumper dangling from the front like a loose tooth.

He pulled Jimmi out of the car, dropped him in the street. He sat on his back, pressed his face into the asphalt and held it there. He turned it back and forth against the road.

"What the fuck are you doing?" Perry said, over and over again. "What the fuck are you doing, Jimmi?"

Alex hit him on the back of the head and Perry rose up. Alex shrank. Jimmi hit Perry again in the back of the head. He hit him in the face, in the stomach, in the ear. He pushed him and Perry collapsed. Jimmi grabbed Perry's hair and wriggled his face over and against the curb, tried to feel for the click of his teeth against the concrete. He brought his foot down.

"Ha!" He exhaled for strength, and to cover up the sound of Perry's face cracking.

It wasn't long before the police arrived. Jimmi and Alex ran, but were caught only a few blocks over. They were arrested together. Alex insisted he'd been a part of it, but Jimmi assured them he had not. He'd done nothing. He was only trying to help his friend. Jimmi was tried and convicted for manslaughter, sentenced to twenty-five years. He was eighteen when he went in.

Alex visited him monthly for the first three years. Joe never once visited. He wrote a letter stating he thought Jimmi needed the time to himself.

As much as I love you, the letter read, *I know, and I know you know, that you deserve this. Life is invaluable, Jimmi. You know that. You've always known that. Remember your snakes? Your frogs? Remember when we were only kids and you managed to get that piece of glass out of my mouth before I cut myself? Remember crying because I was crying because I thought you were trying to hurt me? You were trying to save me. You did save me. Remember that? Remember that, Jimmi, while you're away. I love you.*

Their mother delivered the letter. She could hardly stop crying long enough to speak, long enough to say it was from his brother. She was convinced their family was cursed. She told Jimmi it wasn't his fault. They'd been cursed from the beginning. Their entire bloodline, for years, and for something that had happened so long ago no one could remember what it was, so they would remain cursed forever. Jimmi asked her not to visit anymore. She upset him. He didn't want to see her. He needed to believe things would get better. He needed to believe it wasn't over.

."Don't visit me anymore," he said. "Tell Alex the same."

Alex didn't listen. Not at first. When he got sick, he wasn't able to come as much as he would have liked. Eventually, he was hospitalized. Cancer in his marrow. He had only a few months.

Jimmi met his wife through a letters-to-convicts service, which he enrolled in after fifteen years of incarceration. She asked him about life in prison, about what he'd been like before he went inside. He told her he hadn't known what he wanted. He'd been confused. Things hadn't been easy. Not knowing what he wanted had left him feeling helpless, without guidance or clarity. But that had all changed once he began to lose things. Once he lost his freedom, lost his best friend, his right to a normal life, he knew what he wanted. He wanted those things. He wanted friendship, love, television, cold beers. He wanted people he could rely on. He wanted people who could rely on him. He wanted children, a wife. He wanted to devote himself to something. He wanted to show God he was worth loving. He wanted to be worth loving. When he was finally released, they were married. She was pregnant within a year. They were happy together, though Jimmi was given to fits of melancholy. He put holes in the walls, but never raised his hands to her. He was holding her hand when the baby came.

"She's beautiful," he told his wife. She couldn't hear him. She'd gone still only a few moments after Clara had appeared. "She's perfect," Jimmi said.

When their own mother died, Jimmi flew home, to help his brother with the arrangements.

Joseph had a home in their old neighborhood where he lived with his wife and two daughters. Jimmi and his daughter roomed with Joe for a week while they finalized the details concerning their mother's burial. She was buried on a Sunday, in the morning.

After the funeral, Jimmi's daughter, Clara, asked if his mother and her mother were together now because they had both died. Jimmi said they were. She asked if we all had to die and if he, Dad, was going to die too and Jimmi said, yes, they were all going to die. He was going to die too. But not for a long time, and it wasn't something to be afraid of. She asked why not? Why not be afraid? And he said because life was a very, very, very good thing, and death was a part of it, just like any other part.

"What do you do when a part *is* scary?" she asked.

"Refocus your attention," he said. "Think of something else."

Clara said that, okay, she wasn't afraid, but it made her sad, and Jimmi said that was fine, it made him sad too.

He and Joe spent only a small amount of that week alone together. Joe told a few jokes. Jimmi drank cup after cup of coffee.

"How's Clara?" Joe asked.

"She's good," said Jimmi.

"How are you?" he asked.

"I'm good," said Jimmi.

On the plane ride home, Clara closed her eyes during takeoff and landing.

"I thought you weren't afraid," said Jimmi.

"I'm not," said his daughter. "I'm thinking of something else."

Jimmi read his daughter bedtime stories and the girl sometimes described what she saw.

They were in a two-story apartment, the monkey and the man. Their hands were rounded and stiff, but still able to grip onto things like ladder rungs, which they needed to climb to the second story. The monkey liked records and the man liked CDs. When they weren't on adventures, they did things like climb into a car with their friends and drive to the Great Wall of China. These were fairly quiet trips, fairly normal. Nothing much happened, but they took lots of pictures, and told the stories over and over.

Jimmi's daughter loved preschool. She loved playing with the other kids. She started telling stories all the time to anyone who would listen. She told stories about things she'd heard other people talk about, and filled in what she didn't know.

"My dad hit a squirrel with his car today. Its body was stiff, but his face was smooshed. He got out of the car and picked the squirrel up off the ground and wrapped it in a shirt he'd just picked up from the cleaners. The shirt was so white he could see the squirrel leaking through it, so he put the squirrel and the shirt in the backseat and drove us all home where he buried the squirrel in the shirt in the backyard. He told me it was a nice shirt and the squirrel would like to be buried with it. I said the squirrel would like to be buried with a nut, or *in* a nut. A nut he could eat himself out of. My dad said next time, and I said *what?*, because I wanted him to say it again, and he said *never mind*."

"You told that story at school?" Jimmi asked.

Clara nodded.

"Did you get in trouble?"

She shook her head.

"Cool," Jimmi said. He wrote the story down, and put it on the re-frigerator.

In the park, Jimmi talked to the other parents. The mothers, the fa-thers, the children now and then. Clara and the other kids built an enormous sand castle and disappeared inside of it. The children came out hours later—Jimmi and the other parents were on the bench, pa-tiently waiting—and they looked entirely exhausted. A little older, a little surer of themselves. There was sand in their pockets, in their hair. They weren't able to describe what they'd done, what they'd seen exactly. But they took deep breaths and left with their parents, hand in hand, and none of them were much like they had been before.

Clara asked Jimmi when he was going to find another wife. But Jim-mi didn't want to focus on that, on himself. He wanted to raise his daughter to the best of his abilities, and he would seek out someone when the time was right.

Clara was less social in grade school. She had two best friends, Sam and Susie. They were over every weekend, made forts out of the couch cushions. They draped a canopy roof of bed sheets over the cushions and sat beneath them in the darkness together. They ate bowls of chips and told stories under the canopy. Sam was in love with Clara, anyone could have seen it. Around her, he was red-faced most of the time. He was comfortable, but looked to her for approval for nearly every decision.

"We could angle this pillow, extend this area and make a little kitchen space where we can keep the bag of chips and the crackers, right Clara?"

When they weren't hidden in the fort, Jimmi watched the kid flirt with his daughter, watched him pine away for her, and realized things would get very complicated as she grew up.

One Sunday, Sam asked Jimmi for permission to dig a hole. Clara was in the backyard, and Jimmi was moving about the house, doing Sunday things, checking occasionally on Clara in the yard whenever his fluttering led him from one room to another. Sam knocked and Jimmi came to the door.

"I was thinking of digging a hole," the boy said, "for Clara."

"Okay," Jimmi said. "Do you think that's something she'd like?"

"I don't know," the boy said. "I'm not sure what I'd find."

"You're looking for something?"

"Not exactly."

"What's the use of the hole?"

"It's for Clara," said the boy.

"Right," said Jimmi.

"I would need to borrow your shovel," the boy said. "My parents say they're particular about their tools."

"What if I'm particular about my tools?" asked Jimmi.

"Are you?"

Jimmi thought a moment. He was most interested in what exactly this kid meant. How far would the hole go? What would they use it for? *Where* would it go?

"Where are you going to dig?" Jimmi asked.

"I haven't decided yet."

"Shovel's in the back," Jimmi said. He led the boy through the house, to the backyard. They got the shovel from the garage. Clara waved, started to come over. Sam took the shovel and left.

"Was that Sam?" she asked.

"It was," her father said.

"Did he want to play?"

"He wanted to borrow the shovel."

"Why?"

"To dig."

"Dig what?" she asked.

"I'm not entirely sure," Jimmi said.

The next day Sam began to dig. He wandered deep into the woods. He found a circular clearing and dug in its center. He dug for hours, until he tired, then he rested. He drank water from one of the many bottles he'd brought with him. He went home just after dark, and went back after school the next day. He isolated himself more or less, and his friends began to wonder. His parents wondered less, they assumed he was with his friends.

The hole got deeper. The hole got very deep.

One day, Susie and Clara decided to follow him. After school, he left the building and headed home. He entered his garage, came out a moment later with the shovel in hand. He walked, the shovel's head hanging down, scraping a line in the pavement behind him, until he abandoned the sidewalk for the tall grass. They hung back, watched from behind buildings and houses, bushes and cars. He trailed through the tall grass until he reached the edge of the woods, and he entered them without hesitation. They followed, a little more closely now, less sure of his path, less confident of their ability to anticipate his movement. They turned flat behind trees, they moved on their heels, lightly on the tips of their toes, until finally they reached the clearing. There was a small lamp there, a chair, bottles of water, a basket, and an enormous dark hole. Beside the hole was a raised wheel with a cord of rope dangling from either side, into the hole. Sam lifted the lantern, and walked to the edge of the hole. He crouched and turned, dropped his legs over the edge and disappeared. They waited a moment, a few minutes. They looked at one another. They moved to the hole's edge.

When they looked over, there was only darkness. They could see nothing but the rounded curve of the hole's edge, the dark dirt disappearing. There was no light. Nothing but the two ropes dangling from the wheel and a thin rope ladder hung from the hole's rim, the cords soiled and frayed with use.

They climbed into the hole, Susie after Clara. They lowered themselves slowly, rung after rung. They heard the faint, chunky sounds of Sam digging. Susie did not look down. Clara looked over her shoulder, past her feet, and saw a bit of glitter somewhere in the distance. It moved. It bounced. It turned this way and that, as if alarmed at their approach. Sam set the lantern down, and the light seemed to grow around him.

Sam dug steadily, patiently, dropped the dirt into a bucket at his feet. When the bucket was full, his tired arms gripped the rope that was tied to its handle. He pulled. The bucket lifted. He pulled until the bucket lifted out of sight. He tied the rope to a large white rock they had not noticed before, and he turned toward the rope ladder.

"Hi, Sam," Clara said.

Sam hadn't planned to wait this long before telling his friends about the hole, before showing Clara and explaining it had all been for her. But once he started, he'd been unable to stop. He devised new plans to keep the project going, the rock and pulley for excavating loose dirt, for example. There was always more hole to be dug, he realized, so he kept going.

"Why did you start?" Clara asked. They were sitting around the hole's edge. Sam's feet dangled above the darkness. Clara and Susie sat a few feet back.

Sam looked at the hole for a moment. He looked at Clara.

"Why did I start?"

She nodded. It was twilight. Her pale skin had a bluish hue. Her dark hair looked even darker, nearly black. She wiped her mouth with her wrist.

He shrugged, looked back to the hole.

"Can we help?" asked Susie.

Sam dug and Susie pulled the rope that brought the bucket of dirt up to Clara who carried the bucket off into the woods, where she distributed the contents onto the rising layer of topsoil.

They went on like this for days. They angled the hole so it eventually ran parallel to the earth above it. Susie snuck a shovel and bucket out of her parents' garage and brought them to the dig site. She dug alongside Sam, filled her own bucket as she did. Clara retrieved two buckets at a time, carried them one after the other, out into the woods.

They kept this up for days. They came home covered in mud and cuts and fell almost immediately asleep.

"Where have you kids been going?" asked Jimmi.

They were at the breakfast table. Clara had a scrape on her cheek from the night before. It was swollen, discolored. The bucket's dirty handle had slipped from her hand, and she'd lost her balance, fell against the bucket's edge.

"Just playing in the woods," she said. She ate eggs on bread with bacon and cheese. She mopped up the extra yolk with her crust.

"Does this have to do with why Sam borrowed my shovel?"

Clara thought a moment. She hadn't thought of that bizarre exchange for some time—it seemed somehow unreal.

"Yes," she said. "I guess it does."

"This is impressive," Jimmi said. They'd dug an impressive hole. They'd tunneled into the earth. They had a system. Jimmi bought a few more shovels, told them to invite their friends. Soon they had a team of thirty plus. A long line of diggers and excavators with Sam at the front and Clara at the back. The air was thin at the front of the tunnel, so every now and then Clara, who stood at the edge of the hole, opened her mouth, let it fill with air, then sealed her lips. She pressed her mouth against Sara's. Once their lips were sealed against one another's, Clara opened her mouth just enough for the air to escape. Sara withdrew, her lips sealed. She climbed down the ladder and pressed her mouth against Roy's. They repeated the process. Roy walked a length of the tunnel and pressed his mouth against Jack's. Jack walked a further length of the tunnel and pressed his mouth against Ashley's. Ashley walked a further length of the tunnel and pressed her mouth against Anthony. Anthony walked a length of the tunnel and pressed his mouth against Danny's. Danny walked a length of the tunnel and pressed his mouth again Gauri's. Gauri walked a length of the tunnel and pressed her mouth against Lydia's. This went on until the small pocket of air finally reached Susie, who pressed her mouth against Sam's. Her cheeks went red. Sam thought he could taste Clara.

He hardly ever saw her anymore. He was getting farther and farther away from her, but he could not stop digging. She was there, as nearly everyone else was, to see where this was going.

The children dug for weeks, months. Jimmi, along with a few other parents, brought them food and water and comfortable materials on which they could sit or sleep. The parents watched their children work. It was a fine sight to see, them all working together. How dedicated they were, how focused. Every now and then one of the parents would erupt into a cheer, or begin to applaud wildly. Some cried. One woman said over and over again, "I could not be prouder; I could not be more proud."

Jimmi brought gloves for Clara. He brought her a handkerchief. He held her small hands, which were rough with work.

"Do you mind if I'm here?" he asked. "Do you mind my watching?"

She did not mind, but she had to get back to work. The buckets of earth were coming steadily now, and there was no time to waste if they were going to get as much work done as they could before it was time for dinner, a shower, and bed.

Jimmi did not miss her, not really. But he still felt a sadness at the sight of her working alongside all of her friends. There was nothing he could do to help her. She did not need him here, not really. He could have been home, he realized, preparing a well-rounded dinner, or cleaning her room, which was dusty and streaked with mud. He could have been laying out her clothes, buying her new ones. In a way, it was selfish, his watching her, his admiring her from afar while she carried on, indifferent to his presence. Every now and then, though, when she returned from the woods with an empty bucket, or after she tied the bucket, lowered it over the hole's edge, she would look up, see him there, and she would wave. Just as casually, she would go back to work. But he was left with an immensely pleasurable feeling. He felt wine drunk, happy for her and for him. He felt full of purpose, sitting there on the quilt he'd brought for her, in case she got tired and needed to rest. She never did, though. She never rested. She was one of the hole's hardest workers.

❀

The day the children began to faint, Jimmi had brought egg salad for all the parents, and any child tired enough to rest. Some of the diggers fell first. Then some of the children carrying buckets. One child fell while climbing the ladder. He hit the bottom of the hole with a wet thud. Sam stopped digging when he heard the sounds, wet thuds all around him. He ran the length of the hole, climbed the ladder and said,

"Everybody's falling over."

Parents charged the mouth of the hole. They paced, waited, while a handful climbed down the single rope ladder. Clara returned from the woods to find Jimmi in a panic. He patted her down, touched her arms, her cheeks, the top of her head. He looked into her eyes, snapped his fingers. He blew in her face and she flinched. He fell to his knees and kissed her hands and she asked what was happening.

He didn't know, but some of the children had fallen. They were collapsing. Something was wrong.

"Is it the air?" she asked.

He didn't know.

Only six children fainted. Men carried them out of the hole, draped over their shoulders. They laid them out on the wood floor and ran for help while everyone gathered around them.

"Get back," said one of the parents.

"We need a doctor," said another.

"Somebody get a doctor," said a third.

Jimmi said, "Do you want egg salad? Does anyone want egg salad?"

❧

The children were exhausted. Even those that hadn't fainted. They'd worked and worked and dug themselves a tremendous hole, but they were not able to keep up that rate of production. They'd rested when they'd needed to. They'd eaten well. They took care of themselves. But it was still too much. So they stopped. The hole remained. It could not be called incomplete. It was as much as it had ever been. A hole.

Sam returned Jimmi's shovel. He asked to see Clara.

"Sure," said Jimmi.

Clara was in her room. Jimmi told Sam to wait, he would go and get her.

In her room, Clara on the bed, coloring a stack of computer paper.

"Sam's here."

She looked up. She smiled at her father. He'd given her the computer paper. He'd given her the colored pens.

"I'm bored," she'd said.

When she colored, she did not stop for lines or distinct shapes. She let the pens wander the page. She got ink on her bedspread, ink on her hands. She filled the pages with movement.

"I'm really happy to see more of you at home," he said.

She looked back down at her coloring.

"I was starting to miss you, even though I still saw you every day."

She asked if Sam was coming in and Jimmi said he'd told him to wait a moment.

"I think Sam wants to take you away," Jimmi said.

She stopped coloring. She looked up.

"Take me somewhere else?"

"I think so."

"Can I go?"

"If you want."

"Do I want to?"

Jimmi shrugged.

"I think so," he said.

"Here." She gave him the stack of colored paper.

After she left, he covered the walls of the living room with the paper. It was purple and yellow and red and green and orange and blue and black and white. He phoned some of the neighbors every now and then. Their children were doing fine. He was glad to hear it. He wondered where Clara and Sam had gone, but knew better than to wonder long. There was no way of knowing. And he did not want to know. It was for them, where they went. He would hear from her again. And even if he didn't, he would not forget her.

Her pages wilted in the summer heat. Sun through the windows stained them. He listened to music sometimes. Other times he did not. He started a garden that did not last. He grew much older. He grew a beard. She phoned him one afternoon, while he was sipping lemonade in what had been his garden.

"Hello," said his daughter.

"Hi, sweetie."

A bee landed on the back of his hand. He turned his palm down to consider it, and the bee left.

"Everything is incredible here," she said. "Except we're running low on money."

"Do you want me to send you some?"

She did not answer.

"How's Sam?"

"Sam is Sam," she said.

Jimmi smiled. She sounded happy and confident, like she knew the man so well.

"Sweetie," Jimmi said, "I'm going to die now."

"Okay," she said. "Did you see the bee?"

"Yes," he said. "And thank you."

Clara and Sam did not go far. They bought a horse, and named it

Steel. They adopted a two-year-old girl named Bonnie. They held
Bonnie up in front of Steel and let her touch his nose. The horse
chuffed and Bonnie squealed and hit her hands together.

Their house was small, but on a good amount of land. Sam rode Steel
in the mornings. He filled a barn with wire and cotton and sheet
metal, which he coiled into balls and rolled out to various places in
one of the open fields on their property. Partly so he could jump Steel
over the various obstacles, but mainly because he liked the look of
them. They were gnarled and unfriendly looking from one angle, and
from another they reflected the sky, the grass, the oncoming horse
and rider.

Clara swam in a small pond by the barn. She bathed Bonnie in the
sink. They opened a small store on Main Street. They sold food items,
some souvenirs. Arrowheads and ponchos. They sold peach preserves
Clara made from the orchard she'd discovered the first summer of
their living together. They made just enough money to be comfortable together, and to raise Bonnie. They did not need much. They
lived simply. They ordered food for the store and ate a lot of what they
did not sell. When Sam got sick, Clara ran the store by herself. None
of the customers seemed to mind the young child on her knee, at her
side, on the floor.

They buried Sam on their property, a few yards from the dock leading
out over the pond. A minister came, though they were not religious.
There were very few clouds in the sky. A large puffy one. One that
looked like a star. Clara pointed that cloud out to Bonnie.

"That is your father," she said.

Bonnie squealed, hit her hands together.

At night, Clara told Bonnie stories about Sam, her father. She wanted the child to grow up in his presence, or some semblance of his presence. At first, the stories were mostly true: how they'd met, things they'd done together, the hole they'd dug together, how Sam had proposed, those kinds of things. But Clara began to have vivid dreams, their nights were so peaceful and quiet out on the ranch together, and she weaved elements of those dreams into her stories.

"Your father and I had met many times before we met in this life. We were friends, lovers, teacher and student, we have known each other for many lives." Clara's dreams were startlingly real. She saw herself as practicing the art of lucid dreaming. She pushed for what she considered to be visions, past-life regressions. "I knew your father as a healer in a village many many centuries ago. I went to him. He held my wrist and the pain was lifted."

When she woke from these dreams, in the silver haze that encompassed their ranch home at night, she was always disoriented, confused, frightened, and eventually disappointed. She lived several lives alongside Sam in her dreams, each one just as real as the next. When she woke, she was completely alone.

Bonnie grew older. She lost her teeth. She grew new ones. She was muscular, rugged. She got cuts, bruises, rashes from various plants. She ignored them, and they healed. She learned to brush Steel, and eventually to ride him. By the time she was eight, she was taking early morning rides around the property, into the woods and far out of sight of her mother, who sat on the porch and considered their property with an eye for the familiar. What was truly familiar, anything with which she might feel a connection greater than mere earthly contact. Bonnie arrived home from her rides, sweaty and eager to let the day begin. Steel looked stronger than ever. He was slick with oil and sap from the wooded ride. Bonnie's legs were often littered with cuts. Clara smiled to see them. She took naps throughout the day. She lay in bed, her eyes closed. She waited for the next dream, the next vision. In one, she was a hunter. In one, she witnessed Noah building the ark. She built an ark of her own, along with a team of builders. Sam was there, three nails held between his teeth. They had to hurry, storm clouds were gathering.

Bonnie grew up. She worked regular hours at the store. She attended high school, did well, was well liked. She was driven in almost everything by curiosity. She sought out intimate friendships because she was curious about people. She studied. She read. She rode Steel and explored their property, the surrounding properties. She brought Steel by the front porch, every morning, where Clara would sit and sip water or nothing and wave to her daughter as she disappeared over the hills and into the woods. Clara sat alone and dreamed while Bonnie was out. Clara dreamed she was on the beach, prone in the sand. She rose, walked to the highway. Woods surrounded her. A car approached from behind and pulled over. Sam sat at the wheel. He offered her a ride. A breeze passed through the woods around her and the trees all seemed to shift, to shudder. They leaned into one another. Just then, Bonnie climbed out of the passenger's seat. She looked over at Clara from across the bed of the truck. Clara began to speak, but Bonnie turned. She entered the woods, and disappeared. Clara climbed into what had been Bonnie's seat in the truck. Sam and Clara drove on together. The road, the woods, the car melted away. It was just the two of them, and the sun. They entered the light and fell together. There was little heat. There was wind all around them. Clara felt Sam's hands and the wind and the light of the sun and some part of her finally released. A tension in her shoulders, a tightness she'd been holding for years. Her vertebrae clicked, one by one. She straightened out. She thinned. She vanished.

The woods grew thick around Bonnie. Steel was apprehensive, as she'd never seen him. The trees grew closer together, clung to her legs, Steel's sides. She pushed him on. He paused, she pressed him with her calves. She was not sure anymore, which way was home. The tops of the trees bent toward one another and began to join, to tangle, as if grappling with one another, as if each was trying to pull the other down. She dismounted, took Steel by the reins and led him through the tangled and tangling trees. Finally, she squeezed between the trunks of two enormous cedars, but Steel's shoulders could not fit. He could not move forward. She tied the reins to one of the trees. She told herself she was lost. She told herself she needed to walk on, to continue forward until she reached something recognizable, something familiar.

Eventually, she came upon a hole. A hole in the earth that was darker than the light would go. A rope ladder hung from the edge. Curious, she climbed down. She climbed lower and lower until she was exhausted with climbing. She looked down, but couldn't see a bottom. She only saw the faint light on the walls around her. She could see the vague white of her hands on the ropes in front of her. She saw the ring of light above her. She continued until her arms were weak and she could move no farther. She hung a moment, draped her arms over a rung of the ladder. She breathed a moment. Her knees buckled. She fell.

She hit the ground after only a moment, and collapsed. The dirt was moist. It clung to her arms, her cheeks and hair. She rose up and considered the ring of light above her. There was no way she could climb back up, not right away. Her arms were drained. Her body was sore and frail. She'd been riding, walking, climbing for hours. For what seemed like forever. She patted the walls around her, measured the size of the space. Before she could make a full circle, though, she discovered an opening in the wall, across from where she remembered the ladder being. She kept her right hand on the wall at her side and moved down the corridor. The earth gave beneath her trailing hand. She felt herself dragging slivers into the dirt wall, little canals. She fingered the slick edge of what might have been an earthworm. She felt small roots bend to her touch. She felt the dirt build up beneath her fingernails. She walked on, one heavy step after the next. She thought of her mother. She thought of what it might be like, to live one's life in pursuit of a dream. Not a hope, not a fantasy, but the act of dreaming. An abandonment of one's self to fantasy, to the imagination. For years she had avoided her mother, if only because she felt her mother sought to avoid her. Bonnie rode her horse. She stayed out late, kissed boys, let them touch her, touched them. She stole from their shop, little things, necklaces or candy. Her fingers trailed in the dirt of the wall. She felt disoriented, unsure of each step, but that did not slow her. She walked deeper and deeper. The strength came back to her legs. She felt like she could walk for as long as she would need to, for the entire length of this hole. What she would do then, she did not know. She might sleep. She needed sleep, she knew that. Clara's hand would come up when Bonnie returned. She could walk for as long as she would need to, she knew that. Clara kissed her eyelids, even now. Not every night, but every once in a while. The dirt coiled along her fingertips as she dragged them. She drew clump after clump of raw mud from the wall, dropped them at her feet. She left a little trail of wet clumps. Water dribbled from the holes she made, collected at her feet. Her mother would never be happy, because she believed so wholly in what she could only imagine. Her mind would never shut off the idea of something different, something greater, something holding together all of what little they had. Bonnie felt sorry for her. Bonnie wanted to cry. Step after step, she thought about crying. She moved and the hole seemed to grow with each step. There was no light. She could see nothing at all. Nothing but the textured haze of darkness. Blues and reds, yellows and greens, humming. She was more and more a part of their absence. She couldn't picture light, not exactly. Water lapped the edges of her feet. She remembered Steel. The way he'd looked when she left him. The reins tied to the branch of a cedar tree. The look in his eyes. She'd expected him to look hurt, but he hadn't. His eyes were wet, but they were always wet. He shook the muscles along his back and sides. He pawed at the ground. He looked around, in every direction he was able to turn. She'd walked away from him, looked back once or twice. And he was there each time, looking as he had the moment before, shaking and turning this way and that. He made a few sounds she recognized: a whinny, a chuff. He tapped his teeth. He made one sound she did not recognize, a kind of cough. A kind of sigh or strained breath. She turned and walked in the direction she had set for herself. She took step after heavy step, her hand trailing in the mud, the water coming. His hoof came down, and he curled his leg back up.

Just outside of town, there was a creek. A thin thing, with little

power behind it, hidden beneath a coat of tall grass. Passing by, passing over, one could hear it before it came into view. The sound of running water filled that stretch of land. Though faint, it could be heard for a good distance in any direction. The creek was miles from a hydroelectric dam. The dam had a small leak at its base. Over time, the foundation had shifted, the concrete began to crack. As the crack grew, the foundation weakened. The creek's source was that quarter-inch crack in the foundation of the hydroelectric dam. It wasn't long before the town discovered the leak. But they were losing very little power to it. At the time, it was cheaper to leave the crack, to keep an eye on its growth, rather than to redo the foundation. Cheaper, easier.

They did not really keep an eye on the crack. It grew. It went more or less unnoticed. People flipped switches. They took hot showers. They charged their phones, their computers. They cooked dinners on electric stoves, microwaved gravy and leftovers.

Joe flipped a breaker, the lights in the house went out. He flipped it again, and everything lit. He heard the buzz of the microwave, the glug of the fish tank's filter. His house was empty, the electronics around him hummed.

His house swarmed with insects. He'd left the window open all through the night. He'd left the lights on, the garage door open, and when he'd clicked on the lamp at his bedside that night, the power had shut off completely. The bugs had died down. There was an intense silence all around. His ears roared.

Coming back from flipping the breaker, he found the insects active again. Mayflies and moths, beetles and winged ants, they flew around him, investigated his ears and beard. They landed on his shoulders, his arms. He poured himself a glass of water, considered the plug in the center of the room. Most of his lights and kitchen appliances ran from a single surge protector in the center of the room. Extension cords snaked out and down the hall, splitting off into the rooms that needed lamps, outlets: his bedroom, the bathroom, his study. The fish moved in their tank as the insects did around his kitchen table, in broken figure eights, fast then slow. They pulsed. June bugs struck the table dumbly. They flipped, kicked their ratcheting arms and legs. Their wings buzzed. Joe's family had grown up and out of the house like vines.

After they left, Joe began remodeling the house. He took down a few walls, tried to rewire the bedrooms and the living room. He was "opening the house up" as he put it. But the place was a mess. A tangle of extension cords and dust.

His daughter's rooms he left untouched. There were only a few things left anyway. Sheets, pillows, a few toys they cared so little about they'd been willing to leave them when they left. His wife had taken everything. Everything except for a mirror they'd had mounted to the bedroom wall. That's not to say she didn't try. That's not to say she wasn't making plans to have it removed.

Joe hung clothes from the edges of the mirror. He obscured it with electrical tape, but made sure to use the kind that wouldn't leave streaks.

He was napping when the water trickled in. It came in under the door, soaked into the rug. It made a soft sound as it ran across the wood floor, soaked into the bags of tools he'd left out, the paper towels he'd dropped earlier in the night and let roll to a stop in the middle of what had been the living the room.

A siren sounded when the water was already a foot or so deep. It lifted an end table, knocked it against the bedroom door. Joe sat up in bed, threw his legs over the side and plunged them into the water. He gathered himself into the center of the bed. The flood siren wailed. The water reached the top of the bed and soaked into the sheets, the comforter. It slid over the top of the bed to meet itself in the center. Joe got off the bed and stepped into the water. He knocked smooth objects with his feet. He opened the bedroom door, more water poured in. The house was filling, was full, was empty. He opened the front door and water poured in. He lifted the phone from its receiver, heard nothing, and dropped it into the waist-high water. He realized he hadn't yet made a sound. He screamed, nothing in particular. He just made sound at the water. In response, it rose around him.

Joe had seen images of floods before, and in them, people were always gathered on their rooftops, signaling for help or being saved. He pulled down the hidden ladder to the attic, let it drop into the water. He climbed into the dusty crawl space and made his way to a vent on the far side of the house. The house was empty of insects. They'd abandoned him. He kicked out the vent and it made a soft splash in the water below. He drew his upper body out first, clung to the edge of the roof with both hands. Then he pulled his lower body to the edge of the vent's frame. It bent beneath his feet as he pulled himself up and onto the roof. The shingles scraped his soft, wet feet. He looked out. For miles there was nothing but water, trees, and rooftops. He saw no people, no animals but a few birds. They moved as they always had, indifferent to what was happening below.

Joe sat on the roof. He watched the birds. Only a few passed. He watched the water. It rose, slowly, surely. It grew. He thought of his wife, but didn't know what to think. Maybe she had made it to her roof as well.

The siren wailed. Joe sat on his roof. The water rose, and he yelled.

He yelled and he yelled. But there was no one. He prayed, asked for forgiveness. The water did not stop. If he survived, he would call his wife, his daughters. He would apologize. Not for one thing, but for everything. He didn't know where he would begin, but he would. It was hard to think of one thing in particular that had gone wrong, but things hadn't been right. Joe ignored it, the ever-present feeling that he could be doing something different, *should* be doing something different. He'd never done anything other than what he'd wanted to do, and people had always loved him for it. People had always loved without question, and he couldn't think of a single thing he'd ever done to deserve it. And still, he felt he deserved it. He spent more time alone. The feeling did not go away. And eventually, his wife left. His daughters had been sad, maybe, but they had not fought the decision. They'd cried and packed their bags.

Water filled the gutters, made a thin, metal ringing. He heard the house groan, felt it move, felt it shudder. At first he paced, one far side of the roof to the other. Then he sat, brought his knees to his chest. He put the side of his right wrist against his mouth, spread his lips, and took that part of his arm between his teeth. He sucked his wrist and watched the water rise.

When the water reached the roof, Joe saw a pillow floating just a short distance from him. The pillowcase was white with blue and yellow cartoon flowers. Water lapped the edge of the roof. He rose and went to the roof's edge. Water in every direction. Treetops jutted out, broke the swaying green of the water's surface. There were no more birds. The sun, too, was nearly gone. The sky was golden, but growing dark. It fell to bronze. The water looked dark, darker with each passing moment. He leaned, reached for the pillow, but it was just beyond his fingers. It was dry on top, but gradually retaining water, slowly sinking. He looked around as if a stick or pole might be waiting for him somewhere in an unexamined corner of his barren roof.

He leapt into the water. His head broke the surface and he looked in every direction for the flower pillow. It moved from him with the ripples his body caused. He reached out again, missed, splashed it a bit farther. The sky was dark now, the water too. The pillow went under. He turned himself downward to swim after it. He opened his eyes and could see only the dark gold of the water. He turned, turned again. Nothing. He swam a bit deeper. His cheeks were puffed and rounded with air. He pictured his wife sitting atop the roof of her new apartment complex. She was there in a rocking chair. His daughters would have been at gymnastics practice. Maybe she'd driven to save them. Maybe they were in the car, floating atop the river, on their way to safety. Somewhere near him, the pillow sank deeper. He swam. He reached out for it. He felt he could swim forever.

After the flood, the city repaired the dam. Many made it out just

fine. Others didn't. They rebuilt the city. They rebuilt homes. Some homes. But years later, the place looked better than ever. They added a new movie theater, a water park. They rebuilt the courthouse in the center of the town square.

On the day of the courthouse's completion, the mayor of Gainesville, Kyle Garret, gathered the people together in the square. He lifted the microphone from its stand, surveyed the audience, and began.

"We all suffered a great loss. Losses, really. We lost friends, family, homes. I can't speak to the unimaginable grief we all experienced only a few years ago. But I ask you, on this day, I ask you to remember, that we have not lost everything. You look around you and you see that we have not lost everything. What we've lost will never be forgotten. But we must also remember what we have. We have one another. Look around you. We have a community. We've grown up and out of what might have been the greatest tragedy of our lives. And together, we rebuild. All it takes is the dream," he said, "to rebuild."

It was twilight. Slowly, the streetlights lit. People cheered when the speech ended. They clapped and yelled and embraced one another. Children ran between the legs of their parents. The grass grew. There was an armed robbery and the fireflies stirred. A fight broke out. A condom broke. A man raised his hand and a woman raised her hand. The wheels of the new projectors began to roll. Two strangers fell in love, made coffee. Children filled water guns with urine and someone made a move. Someone clutched her leg, her arm. A movie ended with a confession, with forgiveness, with love. Credits rolled. *Filmed on location*, they said, *in Gainesville, Texas.*

ABOUT THE AUTHOR

Colin Winnette is the author of two previous books, *Revelation* and *Animal Collection*. He lives in San Francisco.

ACKNOWLEDGMENTS

Thanks to my readers and editors, to Andi Winnette, Sara Levine, Adam Levin, Lydia Millet, Jill Riddell, Brian Evenson, Adam Jameson, John Wilmes, Ben Clark, Amelia Gray, Jesse Ball, Jen Gann, and to Scott Teplin, Walter Green, Dan Cafaro, David McNamara, Lacey Dunham, Abby Hess, and everyone else at Atticus Books for their hard work and support. This book is dedicated to my family, with love.